Foreword

The behavior and adventures of the characters
in this book are modeled after those of certain
actual meerkats still living in the Kalahari.
These creatures wish to remain anonymous to
protect their privacy. For this reason,
their names and their language have
been changed. Any similarity between
these characters and any meerkat-stars
of stage or screen is purely coincidental.
Furthermore, any resemblance between
Oolooks or Whevubins on safari, actual
Click-clicks or Sir David Attenborough
is purely in the eye of the beholder.

Ian Whybrow

First edition for the United States published
in 2013 by Barron's Educational Series, Inc.

Text © Ian Whybrow 2011
Illustrations © Sam Hearn 2011

First published in 2011 by
HarperCollins Children's Books
77-85 Fulham Palace Road
Hammersmith, London W6 8JB

All inquiries should be addressed to:
Barron's Educational Series, Inc.
250 Wireless Boulevard
Hauppauge, New York 11788
www.barronseduc.com

ISBN: 978-1-4380-0303-0

Library of Congress Catalog No.: 2012953972

Date of Manufacture: February 2013
Manufactured by: B12V12G, Berryville, VA

Printed in the United States of America
9 8 7 6 5 4 3 2 1

Meerkat Madness

IAN WHYBROW

Illustrated by Sam Hearn

Also available by Ian Whybrow

Little Wolf's Book of Badness

For Judith Bows, Library Supremo, and all the children of ICS, Zurich and especially for Abbie, Lara, and Caroline, who asked me to do an adventure story for them; for Nilou who likes yellow, Esther who likes dark blue, and Maria and Malti who prefer purple.

Mimi

Uncle Fearless

Beginning

Down

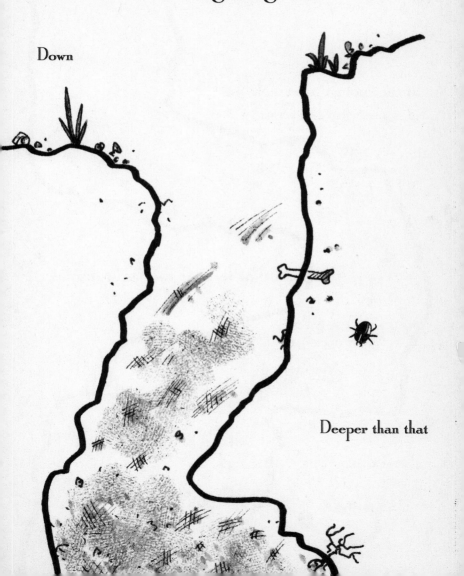

Deeper than that

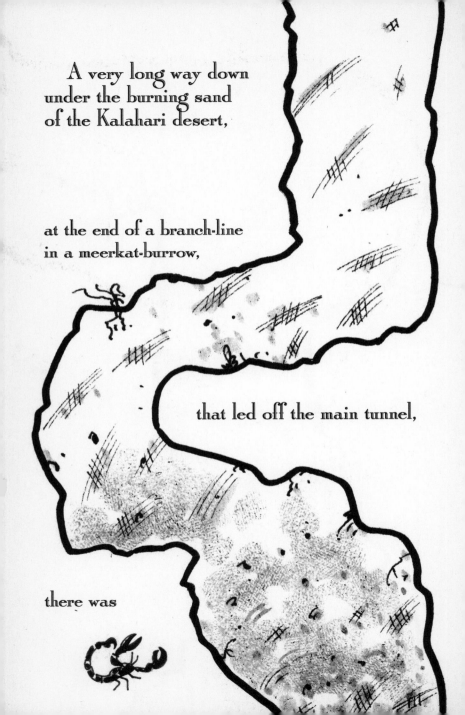

A very long way down
under the burning sand
of the Kalahari desert,

at the end of a branch-line
in a meerkat-burrow,

that led off the main tunnel,

there was

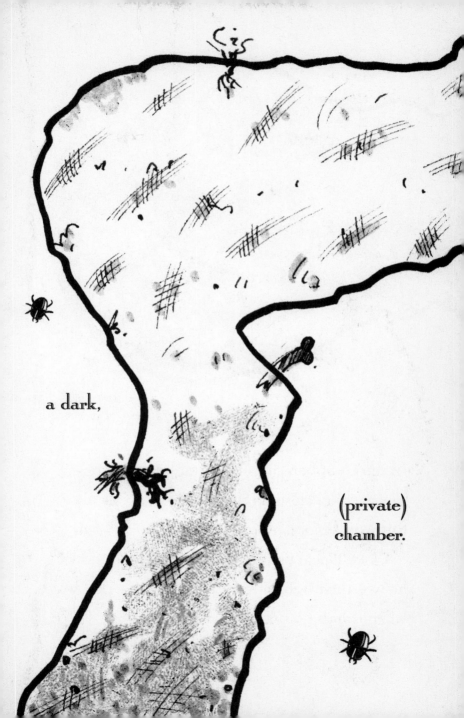

a dark,

(private)
chamber.

In the chamber, three meerkat babies were
squeezed up close on their uncle's lap, because
this was, in fact, a nursery.

Once Uncle Fearless had been a king; now
he was their babysitter. That is the meerkat way
when things go badly.

One of Uncle's eyes was missing and his fur was a bit patchy and ragged in places. His left arm had an unusual bend in it. "War wounds, what-what!" he would often explain. He had not lost his royal pride.

This secret nursery was completely dark. Once or twice Uncle had shown the babies how to dig through the thick sand that served as their main door, but there was no light in the tunnels outside. So, the young meerkats had not yet seen what their uncle looked like.

He had just come down from the Upworld with supper. He hadn't had much time to forage, for a fierce sandstorm was raging outside the safe fortress of the burrow. Still, he had brought them each some worms. And for a treat, there was a plump Flap-Neck Chameleon to share. Delicious!

"Make us big and strong!" piped Little Dream. He was growing fast, but he was by far the smallest of the three. That meant he was always last in line. He was born a moment or two before his brother and sister, Skeema and Mimi, but they had always treated him like the baby. He talked in a strange way, and, to tell the truth, they thought he was a bit dumb.

Uncle wanted the little meerkats to settle down and go to sleep. "For *tomorrow*," he promised them, "you must all be ready to leave the nursery and join the rest of the tribe!"

How they squeaked and squealed and squirmed when they heard that! They weren't at all sure that they wanted to leave the safe and cozy darkness. It wasn't easy for Uncle to calm them down, and he had to use his warning voice before they settled.

"Don't worry," he said. "It'll be fun." He told them that there were some older, more important meerkats in the burrow; some princes and a princess. Now that Skeema,

Mimi, and Little Dream were old enough, he
was ready to lead them along the tunnels to
the Upworld and introduce them. And then,
if they were very good, they would meet the
King and Queen.

"You'll be able to *see* them," said Uncle. "It's
like smelling with your eyes. The sun will show
you how. It's lovely."

"And will we see you?" asked Skeema.

"Oh, yes. As a matter of fact, I look
wonderfully handsome in sunlight," he
answered. The little meerkats weren't sure
what that meant. Still, for the moment they
were happy just to know that he was there
to defend them and that he had a sharp and
special smell that they were very fond of. They
could not remember their mother, Princess
Fragrant. She had been taken by a wild dog
when they were just three days old. They could
just remember Flower, who had nursed them

and fed them milk in the very early times. But it was Uncle whom they loved. Even if he did puff himself up, he meant the world to them.

"Tell Mimi a story," said Mimi, cuddling up. "Me! Me!"

"Not just Mimi. Tell all of us!" begged Skeema.

"Blah-blahs," said Little Dream.

"Yes," said Skeema, "Tell us about the Blah-blahs."

Chapter 1

There was nothing Uncle liked better than to talk about his Glory Days.

He cleared his throat importantly. "Harrumph! This story is called 'The Adventures of Bold King Fearless Among the Blah-blah Tribes,'" he announced.

As usual, the meerkats asked, "Why are they called Blah-blahs, Uncle?"

And as usual he laughed and said, "Because of the funny calls they make to each other, of course! *Blah-blah-blah-blah-blah!*"

They laughed and squirmed happily. Little Dream picked a fat flea off his sister and nibbled it thoughtfully while he listened.

"Now, once upon a suntime," said Uncle, "I left the safety of Far Burrow where I lived, at the far edge of the Land of the Sharpeyes, and set off to explore the Upworld. I wanted to travel and to learn all I could about my kingdom. At first, the rest of the tribe insisted that I took bodyguards with me. I was very precious to them, don't you know!"

"Like me. I'm precious!" Mimi piped up.

"Don't interrupt," said Uncle, holding up a paw in the darkness.

"Why did you need bodyguards?" asked Little Dream.

"Ah, because of the *dangers*!" said Uncle. "Because of the enemies that lurk in every hollow in the sand and under every thorn bush!"

18

"Oh dear," sighed Little Dream.

"Don't forget The Silent Enemy in the sky," added Mimi, who liked to show how clever she was. Uncle gave a trembling twitch and a gasp and she got a sharp nudge in the ribs from Skeema. "Sorry, Uncle!" she exclaimed. "I didn't mean to upset you."

Uncle Fearless took another deep breath to pull himself together. "N-never mind. No harm done," he murmured. It took him a while to calm down, but pretty soon he was happily showing off again. "As I have often told you, it is the meerkat way to stand by one another," he said. "But your old Uncle was not afraid. Oh no, I was young and eager! I said to my subjects: 'I am the greatest of all the Sharpeyes! Do you imagine that I am not brave enough or wise enough to explore my own kingdom *by myself* from time to time if I wish?' And so I ventured out alone, something that you must never, *never* do. Soon I had marked every corner where a meerkat can sniff! I discovered all there was to know out there among the sizzlingly hot Salt Pans at the far end of the kingdom. And do you know the most interesting thing that I discovered?"

"The pointy mounds!" cried the little ones together. They liked this part. "Where the funny Blah-blahs live… *IN THE AIR ABOVE THE GROUND!*"

"Exactly!" cried Uncle. "The Blah-blahs build hollow, pointy mounds, quite close together on TOP of the sand, what-what! Each mound is a burrow for a small tribe. Each mound is taller than a thorn tree; pointy at the top and much wider at the bottom. And do you know," Uncle went on, letting them into the secret, "there's no strength in those mounds at all. The walls are so thin that they ripple in the wind! Isn't that ridiculous? A jackal could tear through those walls in two bites!"

"Ah, but the Blah-blahs are bigger and stronger than us, aren't they, Uncle Fearless?" put in Skeema.

"Oh, yes!" said Uncle. "They're giants. But in many ways they are just like us, only much funnier—and MUCH more charming and cute. I came across several tribes in my travels. Now, who do you want me to tell you about? The Oolooks who always jump up and down when they see a rhino or a giraffe and call *oolook-oolook!* Or would you like to hear about the Whevubins that are always dashing about calling *hurryupp-hurryupp!* when they can't find their young. And when they do find them again, they chase them up and down calling *whevubin- whevubin!*

Little Dream took his thumb out of his mouth and said wetly, "Click-clicks. Tell about you and the Click-clicks."

Uncle scratched his ear with his back leg and he shook so violently that the little meerkats had to hang on tight so as not to fall off his lap. The two biggest ones clung to his chest hair and Little Dream had to keep a good grip on the collar Uncle always wore with great pride.

"Well then, Little Dream," he said. "This collar you can feel around my neck was presented to me as a mark of respect by a very important Blah-blah. He was Chief of the Click-click tribe, no less! I used to see him passing by every day in his Vroom-vroom."

"What's a Vroom-vroom?" asked Mimi.

"Vroom-vrooms are huge, dreadful things!" said Uncle. "How can I explain? Ah, yes... now you all know that meerkats always make sure to dig plenty of escape tunnels when we build a burrow, don't you?" (He felt his little audience nodding away.) "Well, the flimsy mounds where the Blah-blahs live have only one entrance. So they keep special moving burrows nearby and jump into them whenever they sense danger. At the first sign of a lion, a rhino, or any animal that bites or tramples—off they run, *Vroom-vroom!* Those things can move like stampeding wildebeests, what-what!"

"Oh, really, Uncle!" laughed Skeema, not believing a word, but still enjoying the story. "You'll be telling us next that Vroom-vrooms have got legs!"

"Not at all, my boy. They glide along on round spinners that throw up clouds of sand! They do a terrible amount of roaring and dust-kicking and sometimes they let out an alarm call…*Beep-beep!* I'm pretty certain that these are tricks to frighten their enemies. But did your Uncle Fearless jump down the nearest bolthole when he saw them coming?"

"Never! No way!" cheered the meerkats.

"Of course not!" crowed Uncle Fearless. "I stood my ground like a king…"

"And then you *tamed* Chief Click-click!" cried Little Dream, full of admiration.

Skeema rolled his eyes. *It's all made up,* he thought. Still, he didn't want to interrupt a good story.

"Well done, Dreamie! Yes, I tamed him. Mind you, it took ages before he and two of his subjects plucked up the courage to leave the safety of their Vroom-vroom. But finally, they came out. And bit by bit, they moved closer toward me on their tall, tall hind legs. The Chief led the way. He was very shy in spite of his great size, and at first he only dared look at me through the shiny box he held up in front of his eyes to protect them! Sometimes the chief went *click-click!* with his tongue, too, meaning that he was my subject. As each suntime passed, he became bolder and moved a little closer, bringing me tasty gifts of food. In the end, he knelt on the sand in front of me and bowed down—completely tame. "You are my king!"

he seemed to say. I could do what I wanted with him. He even allowed me to climb on to his head and use him as a look-out post."

"Oo! What did he feel like?" gasped Little Dream. "Are they furry like us?"

"Well, let me tell you… When you climb up any of the Blah-blahs you will find that their legs are mostly smooth and warm. They feel dry like bark. Yet on the middle parts of their bodies, they have a covering. It's soft, I would say, not at all furry. Except on their heads. A lot of them have fur on their heads."

"Uncle! Have you *really* climbed a Blah-blah?" said Mimi.

"Oh, many times! Once they know who's boss, they're safe as burrows to be with."

"What did the other Sharpeyes say when you told them?" asked Skeema, giggling. "Did they say, 'Oo, Your Majesty! What a big

27

fibber you are! There's no such things as Blah-blahs or galloping Vroom-vrooms! You're just making this all up.'?"

"Not at all, you saucy young dung beetle!" he boomed. "Most of the tribe were too scared to come out of the burrow at first, but when at last they did, they saw for themselves. Of course, it took a bit of time to get used to the size of the great clumsy creatures, but in the end all the Sharpeyes got to know them. In fact, we did our best to teach the Blah-blahs useful skills. We showed them the way to dig proper burrows, how to forage for food, how to do sentry duty... all that sort of thing. We even showed them how to do a war dance. The sad thing was, the Click-clicks turned out to be a bit boring. They never did much of anything, apart from sitting and hiding behind their eye-protectors."

"I believe all of it," said Little Dream. He never doubted his dear old babysitter.

"Mind you," added Uncle a little sadly, "all this was…Harrumph!…before my…er… accident, of course. I couldn't be a king any more after that. My brother had to take my place."

"Sad," murmured Little Dream.

Suddenly Uncle's fur stood stiff and he was on the alert. "Wup-wup-wup!" he called urgently, and pulled the meerkats tighter to him.

"What is it, Uncle?" whispered Skeema.

"I can feel something! There! The ground's shaking!" said Mimi.

Loose sand began to drift onto them from the ceiling. The three began to cough and whimper.

"Is it an enemy?" whispered Little Dream.

Skeema jumped down from Uncle's lap and darted around the chamber making spitting noises. He always liked to have a plan. His present one was to run to an escape tunnel. He found himself digging furiously at the chamber door to get out.

"It's an earthquake, possibly," said Uncle. "Hush, now, Skeema. Stay with the group."

"*Vroom-vroom!*" breathed Little Dream.

Chapter 2

After a minute or two, it was silent once more.
Uncle sounded the all-clear—*Yee-oh-oo-oo-oo!*—
then he mused, "Do you know, Little Dream,
you may have been right. I suppose it *could*
have been a Vroom-vroom." He paused to
have a sniff and a think. "But I doubt it. They
never come over to this side of the kingdom
of the Sharpeyes. No." He clacked his teeth
together to show that he had made up his
mind. "I think it much more likely that the
sandstorm was playing tricks in the tunnels."

The three meerkats relaxed. As soon as the danger passed, they were asking questions about the Blah-blahs again.

"Do they stand on all fours?" Mimi wanted to know.

And Little Dream asked: "Why they want to hide their eyes all the time?"

"Ha-ha! Good questions! To answer yours first, Mimi: mostly they seem to move on their hind legs. And, as I mentioned before, they're taller than ant hills. Do you remember our lesson, where I taught you all how to stand like sentries?"

"Yes, yes," squeaked the cubs, wriggling and stretching out their hind legs.

"Well that's how the Blah-blahs stand!"

"I can stand!" squealed Little Dream and showed them. It was too dark to see him struggling to balance. Finally he fell on his nose. *Bonk!* The others heard him, but took no notice.

"Do you mean the *she*-Blah-blahs as well as the *he*-Blah-blahs?" Mimi squeaked. "Can the she-Blah-blahs stand? Like Mimi? Like me? Like me?"

"Oh, give yourself a rest!" said Skeema scornfully.

"Yes, Mimi, hush now," said Uncle Fearless. "The Chief of the Click-clicks always has a female with him. Her legs are as long as the trunks of young baobab trees. She has a long, pale mane, but no fur otherwise, and she has longer claws than the male. Sometimes they shine bright like red berries. Her calls are softer than the males, except her alarm calls. Oh my goodness, I remember once when a scorpion scooted right up to her paw! She could easily have pounced on it and sucked the juice out of it. But what did she do? She did a funny sort of war dance and ran away making a noise like a scared baboon—*eee!-eee!-eee!*"

Skeema enjoyed that. "Now make up something funny about the males," he begged.

"He's *not* making it up," insisted Little Dream.

"Ah, yes, I was going to tell Dreamie about their eyes, wasn't I?" said Uncle, ignoring Skeema. "The Blah-blahs look like young meerkats in a way, because their eyes are dark and usually on the front of their faces, but they're flat and square and very shiny."

"What do you mean, *usually on the front?*" asked Skeema. "Can they move them to other parts of their face?"

"Oh, yes. Their eyes are joined to their ears by little arms. So sometimes the Blah-blahs lift their eyes up and put them on top of their heads."

"Oh!" gasped Mimi.

"Oh, yes, they're very strange," said Uncle. "The Blah-blahs' noses are quite small compared to ours, so perhaps they can't smell very well and they depend on their eyes to keep them safe. Their eyes are so dark and shiny that when I first got close to the Chief and he was sitting down, I thought I was looking at a mighty meerkat warrior from a rival tribe! It took me quite a while to realize that I was looking at myself!"

"Vrrrrr!" purred the 'kats, though not all of them quite believed this part.

"Now, now, it's getting late," said Uncle. "We must all get plenty of sleep. We have a big day ahead tomorrow, remember!"

"Oh, please," begged Mimi. "Tell me just one little bit more."

"Just two things," added Skeema.

"Oh, all right. I'll just tell you one or two more things that made us Sharpeyes chuckle and that's *all*. I'll start with one of the Chief's bodyguards. Sometimes he carried a tiny spear and shield with him. I don't know what he was thinking of. It was far too small to protect anyone! And he spent hours squatting down, just scratching the shield with the point of the spear. Very odd! And instead of marking out his territory in the normal way by squirting things with his scent glands, he…"

"He *what*, Uncle?"

"Now you *are* going to think I'm telling you a whopper of a lie. Every now and then he pulled a small box out of his pocket and yelled into it. Honestly!"

The 'kats kicked their little legs and laughed until tears ran down their faces. It made Uncle laugh just to listen to them. "Honestly-hee-hee!" he protested. "I'm not making this up! Oh, I can't wait to lead you up into the sunlight and get your eyes working! I'll teach you trees! Colors! Sky! Dry, white sand and rich, wet sand after the rains! You'll see how a tasty scorpion dances when it's cornered! I'll teach you how to rub the stink-juice off a millipede by dragging it across the sand! Believe me, seeing is almost as much fun as smelling, what-what! Hang on! I must just have another scratch."

"Look out everyone! Here comes another earthquake!" giggled Skeema.

"Help! A flea-storm!" squealed Mimi with a chuckle.

Uncle pretended to have a fierce fight with them—which was just what they wanted. They rolled about the chamber for a while, wrestling, yipping, play-snarling, and snapping.

"Oof! That's enough! You've worn me out!" puffed Uncle, dusting himself down.

"Uncle! Is it easy to climb a Blah-blah?" asked Mimi, wanting more, as usual.

"Oh, as easy as sneezing! I remember one time I was…" Suddenly he was alert and on his back feet again, shaking the little 'kats onto the floor. "There! You almost got me started again!" he said with a laugh. "But it's *way* past your bedtime."

He rolled them into a bundle and stood over them in the guard position, growling gently but firmly. "No more talk. Busy day tomorrow. There are *so* many lessons for you to learn— you're going to need all your strength."

Chapter 3

The pups were very excited and also rather nervous. Still, they slept soundly.

Fearless was not so lucky. He was troubled by his usual nightmare. He dreamed of beaks and claws and fighting and falling. He flung out his arms and legs like a star. This always happened just at the moment when a giant eagle owl dropped him and left him falling toward the rocks. His jerking, kicking, and shouts of terror shocked him awake—and woke everyone else.

Little Dream was the first to comfort him. "Safe, Uncle," he said, and held him tight. He groomed him for a moment, feeling through his fur for fleas. As soon as Skeema and Mimi realized what was wrong, they were up and hugging him, too.

"I don't know what all this fuss is about," grumbled Uncle, trying to pretend nothing had happened, but trembling all the same.

"If The Silent Enemy comes down on us when we reach the Upworld, I'm going to bite his head off!" said Skeema, doing his best to sound brave.

"Good boy!" said Uncle. "That's the spirit! But don't you worry about enemies. We shall be perfectly safe so long as we look out for one

40

another. You see, I was…well, I was on my own. I was caught off guard, what-what! It was hunger that did it. My mind was on a tasty rock lizard, d'you see? The eagle owl saw his chance, came out of the sun, snatched me into the air, and took out my eye with his claw."

"Poor Uncle," said Little Dream.

"Never be off your guard!" warned Uncle. His voice grew stronger as he added: "Ah! But at least I gave him a taste of his own medicine! I pulled a great mouthful of feathers out of his chest! Ha-ha! That shook him! That showed him who was boss! He couldn't hold me then, what-what!"

He decided not to mention that the eagle owl had dropped him from a great height and smashed several of his bones. This was not the time. He took a deep breath to stop himself from shaking at the memory of it. "But it was all rather a shock, I don't mind telling you. It took me a very long time to get my strength back," he went on. "My mind wandered. I was feverish! I was weak as a grub! The rest of the Sharpeyes thought I had the Meerkat Madness. They didn't think I'd live. So naturally, they had to choose another…"

He couldn't bring himself to finish the sentence and so Little Dream said, "Never mind. You can be our secret king."

"Hear, hear!" cried Skeema and Mimi. "Three cheers for our secret king!"

"Harrumph!" grunted Uncle, feeling foolish. "No more nonsense, now! Up and follow, 'kats. Up and follow." Without another word, he began digging at the nursery door.

The little meerkats had learned their lessons well and stood in line behind him in their digging order. Each passed the scooped-out sand to the one behind, as if they were passing buckets of water to put out a fire. Skeema was right behind Uncle Fearless, his brave heart pounding; then Mimi, then Little Dream. In a flash they had removed more pounds of sand than all their weight put together—and found themselves in a damp and chilly passageway.

Blindly they followed their noses and ears through this and other passages, and into a wider space. Uncle told them in a whisper that they had reached the main tunnel. There were strange, new smells in each place they came to and their paws were tickled by unknown dung beetles at work with their loads.

"On," said Uncle. "And say nothing until I tell you."

They followed silently until the tunnel did a peculiar thing. Its blackness rolled back and became something else, not so solid. This made them gasp and Dream began to whimper quietly.

"Don't worry. This is just the sunlight pushing in," said Uncle. "It creeps into the burrow slowly so as not to shock our eyes. You'll notice it grow bigger as we get closer to the Upworld. But it won't harm us. It'll warm us up and make us feel energized. Then you will understand what we call 'seeing.' You'll enjoy it once you're used to it."

They pressed forward and smelled new air as the darkness began to move aside for a stronger kind of light that made the 'kats eyes

blink. It was there in the half-darkness that
Chancer surprised them. His smell slid out of
a side-tunnel first. Then came his slick head.
That was finally followed by the swaying body
of the King of the Sharpeyes himself.

"Welcome to the Upworld, brother Fearless!"
said Chancer. He didn't *sound* very welcoming.
"The Queen's hungry," he went on. "She's keen
to forage on the hunting grounds, but she is
waiting to greet the young ones at the entrance
to the burrow. So hurry. Come this way. "

Chapter 4

Queen Heartless was nibbling a grasshopper
when Fragrant's little meerkats and their
babysitter were bundled into her presence.
She was waiting on The Spoil, the loose sand
heaped up just in front of the main entrance.
Fearless had once been her husband, but after
his "accident" with The Silent Enemy she had
taken Chancer, Fearless's younger brother, as
her new husband. Chancer ruled the Sharpeyes
with Queen Heartless now. He was the father of
her young royal meerkats.

Queen Heartless hardly glanced at Fearless. He meant nothing to her anymore. That was the meerkat way. It was something he simply had to accept. Still, if it was painful for him to be no more than a babysitter, he did his best not to show it.

The Queen puffed up her fine, pale fur and sat up proudly, staring into the sun. Her back was to the newcomers as they crept, blinking, out of the burrow. The royal pups, Princes Spiteful, Needleclaw, and Snatch, stood beside her with Princess Dangerous. A little way off, the rest of the tribe stood at attention or bobbed busily, scanning the skies and the sands all around for enemies.

The sun was still low in the sky, so the eyes of Skeema, Mimi, and Little Dream were dazzled. Their first sight in this amazing new

Upworld was of something shockingly bright and yellow-orange.

*

For a second, poor Little Dream thought that the Queen must be the sun itself. It hurt his eyes to look at her and he had to turn away. Most meerkats have dark patches around their deep-set eyes that allow them to look directly into the sun without damage to their sight. This was not so for Little Dream. He was born with eye patches that were so pale they could hardly be seen at all. The royal family were quick to notice this and Princess Dangerous could not stop herself from giggling. "Look at that one! Have you ever *seen* such silly eyes!" she whispered.

Skeema and Mimi looked dazed. They felt weak and chilly. Uncle had told them about the need to warm up their tummy-pads by standing in the sunshine, and they tried to stand at attention as they knew they had to. Unfortunately, the journey through the tunnels had made them very tired and they wobbled and fell over. There was more laughter, this time from Prince Needleclaw.

The queen stopped nibbling for a moment. The grasshopper was still wriggling, although she had just chewed its head off. "Have the new meerkats been marked?" she asked the King.

"Stand still," ordered King Chancer, and sprayed them with the royal smell.

FFFT~

    FFFT~

        FFFT!

Queen Heartless-the-Dazzling looked down her long and elegant nose at her damp new subjects.

"Now you share our Sharpeyes' burrow," she announced coldly.

Now you share our Sharpeyes' smell.

Now and forever you are Sharpeyes!

"Repeat after me the Sharpeye motto: *Stay alert to stay alive. And stay with the group.*"

"*Stay alert to stay alive,*" repeated Skeema, Mimi, and Little Dream. "*And stay with the group.*"

"You may now bow and scrape."

They copied Uncle Fearless as he bowed and scraped and licked the royal face and fur, the Queen's first, then the King's. "Now you must greet the princes and the princess," whispered Uncle. It turned out that the royal pups didn't want to be licked. Instead, they formed a noisy gang and rolled the visitors over. Since they were much larger than Skeema, Mimi, and Little Dream, they could do it easily. They went for Skeema first,

snapping and snarling and turning him on
his back in the hot sand. This caught Skeema
completely by surprise. Still, he began to give
as good as he got, returning with interest the
bites and scratches he was given.

Uncle Fearless managed to get in among
the scrapping bodies and whisper into his ear:
"Give way, Skeema! Remember your place!"

Then it was Mimi's turn to be knocked about, and finally, Little Dream's. Mimi was bitten quite hard, but did her best to be brave and not make a fuss. Apart from Uncle, not one of the rest of the watching Sharpeyes moved or said a word.

When the royal meerkats turned on Little Dream, he let out a warning call and words started to tumble out of him: "*Wup-wup-wup*! Don't you pick on me or you'll upset Bold Uncle Fearless—and he doesn't like bad manners! He's our secret king and once he bit The Silent Enemy!"

"How dare you speak to us like that!" sputtered Princess Dangerous.

Little Dream took no notice. "*And* he is the King of the Click-clicks!" he went on. "And he's not scared of Vroom-vrooms, and he can stand on a Blah-blah's head, so you be careful!" It was the longest speech he had ever made.

A dreadful hush fell. This was unheard of!
A meerkat—a commoner meerkat at that—
speaking up without an invitation! In front of
Her Majesty! Some of the humbler Sharpeyes
began to murmur.

"Who does that 'kat think he is?"

"He must be crazy!"

"It's all that Fearless's fault, putting ideas
into his head! Secret king, indeed!"

"Yes, because he had The Madness
himself—remember?"

"You're right! Do you remember the time,
just after the eagle owl attacked him and
dropped him on his head? He twitched, he was
helpless… he talked nonsense, poor 'kat."

"Such a shame!"

The Queen silenced them all with a sharp
cry. Nobody moved. She returned for a moment
to her grasshopper, snapping off the legs one

by one. For a moment there was no other sound except the whirring of insect wings. Then she said, "I have no time for any more nonsense. Tell me, Fearless, are you or any of these 'kats likely to be a danger to me or to my tribe?"

"N-n-not at all, Your Majesty." Fearless was flustered but trying to seem steady.

"A babysitter's job is to mind babies," she said. "Not to fill their heads with nonsense. Mind them. Teach them how to be useful and how to obey. Anything else is… unwelcome. Do you understand?"

"Absolutely, Your Majesty. I—"

"Chancer, children, come!" she interrupted. "I lost more weight in the darktime than is good for me. I must forage for food without delay."

With that, she turned and galloped off toward the hunting grounds.

Chapter 5

"I say, look here, my dear young Dreamer," said Uncle as they stood alone by the burrow entrance on the very edge of the Upworld. "You mustn't go about saying that I'm your... your actual *king*. I mean it's awfully kind of you but it's just not done."

"Ah, but we *like* you being our king," said Little Dream. Small flurries of hot sand blown on the wind made him stagger and squint. Luckily, nature had fitted him with little wind screen wipers, so the sand in his eyes was quickly flicked away.

"It was supposed to be a *secret*, Dreamie, you bedbug! You're not supposed to tell anybody secrets!" scolded Skeema. He turned to Uncle, who was looking ruffled and uncomfortable. "Don't worry, we won't *say* you're our king out loud, we'll just know it," he assured him, anxious to make him feel better about himself.

"Hear, hear!" said Mimi. "You can keep being my secret king too. Now could you teach me the Warm-up, pleeeeease. I'm freezing!"

Uncle Fearless looked at his loyal, brave, and shivering secret subjects and his one eye filled with tears.

"Harrrrumph!" he said, wiping them away with the back of his paw. "No more nonsense. Stand by me and watch carefully. This is how we Sharpeyes do the Warm-up. It's very important that you get it right. Meerkats lose a lot of their strength keeping warm in the burrow in the darktime. When we come up here at suntime, we need to forage and feed. To forage well, we need to be quick. And to be quick, we do—*this*. Hup!" He put his front paws under his big fat tummy and heaved up his black tummy-pad so that it soaked up the sun's rays.

"Hup!" giggled Skeema, Mimi, and Little Dream, pretending that they had big fat tummies to pull up and falling flat on their backs.

"Quiet, you silly kids!" roared Uncle, pretending to be furious. "Warm up properly or you won't get any breakfast!"

The 'kats first foraging trip in the Upworld was so exciting that Skeema and Mimi completely forgot about the coldness of King Chancer and Queen Heartless and their horrid, spoiled, royal 'kats. They were out of sight of the burrow by the Grove of the Prickly

Shrubs. The late summer rains had caused grasses and bright, sweet-smelling flowers to shoot up everywhere, but they didn't notice. They had food on their minds.

Uncle showed them how to sniff for damp sand under the hot, dry top-sand. This was where delicious snacks crawled and tunneled, just asking to be dug out and snapped up. Skeema and Mimi worked a little apart from each other, scrabbling with their front paws and heaving up a mound of sand behind them as if they'd done it all their lives. They found larvae and beetles a plenty. It was terribly exciting, like finding buried treasure, and their squeaks and chatter filled the morning air. Even so, they understood that they were never to get so excited as to have both their heads down at once. While one was digging, the other had to look around for danger.

If the bigger 'kats were quick learners, Little
Dream wasn't quite so confident. Uncle fed
him a couple of sandworms to keep him going,
and then took him a little way away, up the
slope of a sand dune, through the Whispering
Grasses, until they were standing not far from
Leaning Camelthorn. Suddenly Little Dream
dropped flat. "Enemies!" he hissed.

"Don't worry," Uncle told him. "Those
are antelopes. They just feed on grass—oh,
and those really big ones? Those are blue
wildebeest. They won't hurt you either, not
unless they stand on you. Come on. I'm going
to show you High Guarding."

Patiently, he nursed the nervous little
meerkat up the leaning trunk of the ancient
tree and onto the branch above. "Keep going,"
he urged. Up they went to the next branch,
then the next. "Look down there and you can

see Skeema and Mimi on The Spoil, by the birth-burrow entrance. Yes? Now look right over there. You see those hills where the sky ends? Somewhere on the other side of them is Far Burrow. Now turn this way. Can you see Bolthole Sands where the rest of the tribe is foraging? There are plenty of places to run to if an enemy comes, what-what! Now, look at those trees just beyond. What do you see?"

He was pointing to a small forest of black thorns. Some of them had grown into quite tall trees. A few vultures had gathered in a line on the lower branches. Right at the top, a martial eagle was gazing about.

"Don't worry about the droopy ones, the vultures," whispered Uncle. "But keep an eye on that eagle. He's one of our worst enem—" And that was when Little Dream fell off his perch.

Uncle climbed down, looked him over, helped him up to his post, and got him settled. The wind blew, just a little bit. Little Dream's branch swayed, just a little bit.

He fell off.

He climbed up. He wobbled.

He fell off again.

Luckily he fell into soft sand every time, so he wasn't hurt at all and Uncle kept encouraging him. "Up. Straighten your back! Tail stiff and steady. That's it! Now—paws together. Bravo! You've got it, boy!" he called.

Little Dream wobbled. Tail up… Miracle! He clung on. At last— hooray!

"Well done," said Uncle. "Now, let's practice our calls. Remember to keep chirping the all-clear if there's no danger. Off you go, if you can remember it."

"Um, is it *Ee-oo-oo Ooo-oo-oo?*" asked Little Dream timidly.

"That'll do nicely," said Uncle. "Keep it up. And keep watching all around because I've only got the one eye, what-what!"

Mimi had almost disappeared under the sand to the side of The Spoil, and suddenly she was up on the surface, tossing something in her paws. "Look! I've caught something, Uncle! Aren't I clever? What *is* this? Wheee! It's so wiggly! But I'm even more wiggly! Look!"

"Oh, stop showing off," came Skeema's growly voice. "Just eat the thing."

Mimi made an annoyed face, but she was too hungry to argue with her brother. She dug

62

into her snack instead and planned to get him back later.

"Well done, Mimi. You're learning. There's a time to snap and a time to chew. Looks like you've found yourself a gecko," called Uncle. "Eat it up. Geckos have very juicy eyeballs. Yum-yum!"

The thought of something so delicious was too much for Little Dream, who was feeling rather excited himself. *"Yyippp!-Yyippp! Yyippp!-Yyippp!"* he yelled.

Uncle Fearless stiffened and then immediately scampered among the branches like a frantic squirrel. "ACTION STATIONS!" he shrieked. "AIR ATTACK! EAGLE OWL COMING IN! BOLTHOLE! BOLTHOLE! RUN-RUN-RUN!"

He knocked Little Dream off his perch, got behind him as soon as he hit the sand, bit his bottom, shoved him along with his nose, and zipped after Skeema and Mimi, who were both running in circles on the sand.

"DON'T PANIC!" Uncle yelled (though there was a touch of panic in his voice). "GO LEFT! LEFT! NOT THAT WAY! BY THE ROCK! THAT'S IT! DIVE-DIVE-DIVE!" And down the bolthole everyone darted at last.

They panted. They held their breath together to listen, but they couldn't hear anything. They peeped out, but couldn't see anything. There was no sign of a single bird in the wide blue sky, let alone an eagle owl!

"I can't see any sign of danger, Dreamer, old boy. What was it you spotted?"

"Um, I didn't spot anything," muttered Little Dream "You said gecko eyeballs. I got excited."

"What? I... You... got EXCITED?!" spluttered Uncle. "But you were on guard! You

64

were our eyes and ears! You mustn't sound the Eagle-Owl Alarm every time you get a bit excited! You nearly gave me a heart attack."

"Nitwit!" complained Skeema. "You know eagle owls make Uncle panic!"

"Panic? Me? I wasn't panicking!" blustered Uncle.

"You made me drop my gecko!" moaned Mimi.

"Alright, you two!" growled Uncle. "You can be quiet! You didn't put on much of a show yourselves just now! Dashing about in circles like a couple of bushbabies! What did I tell you? Always check for a bolthole *before* you get your heads down."

Skeema could see how much his careless words had upset Uncle Fearless. When he remembered how much damage the beak and claw of an eagle owl had done to him, he felt ashamed of himself. He went over and rolled at Uncle's feet to show he was sorry.

Uncle accepted the apology. Then he noticed that all the pups were looking crestfallen. "Ah, now look here. Come on, cheer up everyone. We're all still alive, aren't we? We've learned a few more survival skills, what-what! All good experience. Well done. Perfect! Just remember, now: '*Danger up and danger down. Clever 'kats check all around!*' Everyone got that? Good. Breakfast here we come!"

"Whirrrr-wee-ooo!" cried the pups with enthusiasm. Up went the rusty tip of Uncle's tail. It waved like a flag and led them off like lightning back to their hunting ground.

Chapter 6

The next suntime, the pups stood with the rest
of the tribe at Warm-up and they all did it
very well. Secretly, Mimi and Skeema hoped
for a word of praise from the King or Queen,
but they got nothing but a squirt from King
Chancer and icy looks from Queen Heartless.
The royal pups were positively rude. They said
they were of no importance at all. They called
them babies and tenderpaws.

Once again the whole tribe dashed off to
the hunting grounds, leaving Uncle Fearless
to teach his group their lessons by themselves

near the entrance to the burrow. He decided to give Skeema and Mimi some look-out practice, so off they raced to Leaning Camelthorn and scampered to the top. Meanwhile, he took Little Dream a little way beyond The Spoil to demonstrate some of the finer points of foraging.

Little Dream sniffed at the hot, dry white sand.

"The food worth a chase

Lives in a damp place," he said, repeating one of Uncle's lessons.

"Quite right. And where's the dampness? Under the surface, yes? Well, come on, young scrabbler, get your claws into it! You must be hungry."

Little Dream *was* hungry and he dug as hard as he could. The soft white sand flew like dust and soon his paw-pads felt the cool, moist, yellower stuff underneath. Uncle's head bobbed up and down to make sure that no four-legged enemy surprised them. "Keep contact! Keep calling!" he told Skeema and Mimi, who were doing a nice job up the tree. Soon Little Dream dug out his first creepy-crawly and dug in. He loved the way it tickled going down his throat. Ahhh! He smacked his lips. He felt stronger already. Into the sand went his digging claws.

"Did I ever tell you about the time the tribe was surrounded by Ruddertail warriors, out on the Plain of the Antelopes?" began Uncle.

Little Dream dug away, too interested in finding food to listen.

"Big meerkats, they were, with eee-NOR-mously long tails," Uncle continued, as if Little Dream were fascinated. "Turned on us, they did! They outnumbered us three to one! The brutes thought they could take over one of our best boltholes. You should have heard their war cries. And the teeth on them! Yet we Sharpeyes stood firm. I remember, I got up on a mound, a tall ant hill it was... or was it a shepherd tree? Aghhh!—can't quite remember. Anyway, whatever it was, I got up it. Frightfully high, it was. I let out a war cry of my own..."

Up in the branches of the Camelthorn tree, without taking her eyes off the skies for a moment, Mimi giggled and whispered to Skeema. "Listen to Uncle," she whispered. "He's going on about his Glory Days again!"

"I'm sure he makes it all up!" whispered Skeema.

Uncle's voice grew louder. "...so I said to my troops, I said, 'Tails up for King Fearless, my men and women! Show 'em your teeth and show 'em the Sharpeye WAR DANCE!'"

Uncle was getting really excited now. He sang and he danced, jumping up and down on his hind legs, head up, fur bristling, showing his fine yellow teeth. "The Chief of the Click-clicks was *very* impressed by this one too, I can tell you!" he said, really getting into it. "Oh, yes. I remember him watching me. He was *terrified*! He stood still as a stick, hoping his eye-protectors would keep him safe, the silly great termite heap!" Soon Uncle was wobbling his bottom about and trying to remember some of the trickier steps. "Now, let me see, how did it go?

"Bouncy-bouncy!

Boom-boom! Call!

Stand-up! Tail-up!

Make-yourself-tall!

Head-butt! Head-butt!

Strike like a snake!

Spit-spit-spit-spit!

Shaky-shake-SHAKE!"

Mimi and Skeema nearly fell off their branches laughing.

Luckily, Uncle Fearless didn't notice, because just at that moment, Little Dream uncovered his first—very angry, very poisonous—scorpion.

"Wh…wh…what do I do?" squeaked Little Dream.

"Bravo, my young hunter!" he exclaimed. "You've hit the jackpot! And talking of war dances—here's a fellow with a very interesting dance of his own, what-what!"

Little Dream peered closely as the scorpion turned his back on him.

"Watch out!" warned Uncle. "He'll have you with that big stinger on his tail if you're not quick!"

Too late! The scorpion moved like lightning. It did a scuffling little shimmy, turned its back, and brought his nasty curved claw down right onto Little Dream's tender nose!

"Yow! He bit me!" screamed Little Dream.

"Then go after him and bite him back!" roared Uncle.

Skeema and Mimi saw what was happening and started screeching. "Eee-eee! He's going to die!" they cried from above. "Help him, Uncle!"

"Stay at your posts, keep the all-clear sounding, and keep a sharp look-out!" barked Uncle. "Leave our Dreamer alone to learn the scorpion dance. Come on, Little Dream, back-and-forth, back-and-forth, and dodge his stinger. Now go for him! Snap his tail off before he stings you again."

Little Dream rubbed his nose and looked at the angry scorpion. It skipped, skidded around like a crazy little bumper car, skipped sideways, backward, forward, all the time waving its poisoned weapon.

"You're all right! He can give you a nasty nip but his poison can't kill a meerkat," Uncle told Little Dream. "Go after him. Quick and tricky wins the game!"

Little Dream began to growl, "Krrrr-Krrr!" He watched the scorpion closely. When he got close, the scorpion struck. This time it missed. "Ha-ha!" cried Little Dream. He moved in— and back. He stepped sideways—dodged the sting—stepped back. Forward. Missed! "Look! Watch me dancing!" cried Little Dream. And when the scorpion lunged at his nose once more, he bit off the stinger, grabbed its body in his jaws, and took a big, juicy bite. "Mmmm!" he murmured. "Yummy!"

It was the most delicious thing he'd ever tasted.

High overhead, too high just now to dive and strike, The Silent Enemy circled and noted what was going on. He could feel the tightness of the scar left by a shocking bite from the very meerkat he was watching, and the sight had spoiled the perfect smoothness of his feathers. Some lifted like porcupine bristles where they should have lain smoothly.

Fearless stiffened and shuddered as he heard the distant, mocking hoots of the eagle owl. "*Hoo-hoo yu-hu-hu-hoooh!*" He guessed what they meant. "You just wait! You will pay for what you-hoo-hoo did to me-he-he! I'll have your other eye-hi-hi!"

Chapter 7

The 'kats continued to work very hard at their studies. By their third suntime in the Upworld, they could all do Warm-up without wobbling or falling over—even Little Dream. They were much better at high and low guarding and foraging for themselves. They got better at grooming and searching one another for ticks and fleas, and they had learned to defend themselves from the surprise play-attacks of older pups. They looked like Sharpeyes, the king made sure they smelled like Sharpeyes, but they still didn't really feel that they were wanted by the rest of the tribe.

Skeema was bored. He was anxious to get away from the entrance to the burrow and do some exploring far away. "When are we going to have some adventures like you, Uncle?" he kept asking impatiently.

"Oh, soon," Fearless said in a vague sort of way. "Once you've learned all the ways of the tribe."

"Bor-ing!" muttered Skeema under his breath.

By now they had wandered over to a dune of dazzling white sand. It was steep and towered over them like a great wave. It must have been formed by the sandstorm that they had heard while they were still living in the nursery chamber. Its side felt hot, even to padded little feet, and so soft that it ran down like water at the least disturbance. Playfully,

Little Dream began to burrow, pulling away like crazy with his front paws.

"Pack it in!" cried Skeema, turning his bad temper on him.

"Don't be so silly, Dreamie!" snapped Mimi, joining in. "There's nothing in there. It's much too dry for foraging!"

"*You* say, Uncle!" said Little Dream. "You say, *No, my subject! Stand still, I command you! Obey your king! Stop that digging or you will feel the points of my teeth!*"

Uncle couldn't help smiling just a little. "Now look here, Dreamie, old boy," he said. "Be sensible and, er, let's all move along and find a bit of shade. It's much too hot to…"

He noticed that Little Dream had stopped listening and was digging more frantically, if anything. "Come along, now, Little Dream!" Uncle said. "We mustn't stay out in the open too long. Do as I say, now. Seriously, this is a command. I'm ordering you now…"

Little Dream's head came up for air. "I can smell something!" he panted excitedly.

"Leave it, Dreamie," said Uncle. "There's a good 'kat."

"Something big," said Little Dream. "Look!"

At first, just a corner of the something came to light. It was shiny pink and had a hard shell. Little Dream's sharp claws could only skid over the surface of it, making a hollow sound.

"Hey! Dreamer's found a tortoise!" said Mimi, excitedly. "Let Mimi help you! Me! me!"

She tried to push Skeema out of the way but he was eager to dig too. So was Uncle Fearless. It was time to use his king voice. "Stand back!" he commanded.

Instantly, the pups obeyed. "Stand guard!" he ordered. They stood to attention, glancing

79

about like the Old Guard. Uncle took a deep breath and hauled sand like the master-digger he was. "If it's a tortoise, it's the biggest one I've ever seen, what-what!" he puffed, as he kept digging. "I need help here. Bob and dig, bob and dig!"

"Aye, aye, Your Majesty!" said Little Dream. This was just the way he wanted life to be.

Many claws make light work and in no time at all, whatever it was lay big, oblong, pink, and strange, sideways on the stony sand.

"Is it just a big shell, Uncle?" asked Mimi. "Or do we have to turn it over to get at the meat?" She brushed accidentally against one of the round spinners on its feet, which made a dull whirring sound as it whizzed around. She yelped and jumped back.

She couldn't help it. She let out the general alarm call: "Wai-wow-wik-wak!"

Skeema laughed. "Don't make such a fuss, Mimi!" he scoffed. "It won't trample you. It's not really an elephant, is it, Uncle?"

Little Dream placed a paw on the shell. His eyes were shining. "Vrrroom-vroom!" he said.

Chapter 8

Uncle walked gravely around the large pink object that Little Dream had discovered. His nose and his one eye got busy.

"Hmmm. Look at the pinkness of it," he murmured. "Why is it pretending to be an elephant? Ridiculous! There aren't any pink elephants in the Kingdom of the Sharpeyes." He sniffed deeply. "Aha, I can smell something! It's very faint, but I'm sure there's a hint of Blah-blah scent here," he declared. "And where have I seen round spinners like this before?" he wondered.

"The sandstorm!" exclaimed Little Dream. "We heard that *vroom-vroom* noise!"

"So we did, by all that's juicy!" cried Uncle. "So that *was* the sound we heard on the night of the storm! The Blah-blahs must have been using a Vroom-vroom to get away from the storm!" He had a thought. "Wait! Keep alert!" Suddenly he was racing up to the top of the ridge again.

He moved along it, bobbing up and down, twisting his neck to point his one eye, always on the look-out. He could see Black Thorn Hill where some of the tribe were going about their business. Some were still foraging and others were taking a nap in the shade. But Uncle had something else on his mind.

"I've found tracks!" he called down to the pups, "...and here! Tracks, side by side! You're right, Little Dream! A Vroom-vroom certainly did come along this way. But why here? They usually stay over by the Salt Pans on the far side of the kingdom. There have never been any of them this close to the birth-burrow!"

"Perhaps it got lost in the storm—because of all the flying sand and stones," suggested Skeema.

"Good thinking, my clever young 'kat!" exclaimed Uncle and scrambled down the slope again. "Let me take a closer look at this thing. Mind out, Little Dream. That's a royal command, by the way!" He gave him a wink. He hadn't felt so lively and excited for ages.

Mimi had found a ring sticking out from one end of the shell. She tugged at it playfully. A long strap stretched out and then snapped back. She ran behind Uncle for protection.

"How big are Vroom-vrooms?" asked Skeema, wondering if this was one.

"Oh, massive!" said Uncle. "Much bigger than this. The ones I saw, you could get a whole tribe of four or five Blah-blahs inside them."

"Well, maybe this shell is a special nursery chamber!" said Skeema. "Maybe the Vroom-vroom we heard was carrying it to a safe place. But then it dropped it by mistake and the storm covered it with sand!"

"A nursery chamber… of course! Brilliant!" exclaimed Uncle.

"But there's no way in or out of it," Mimi said, peeping out from behind Uncle. "If you want to know what I think… *I* think it's an elephant's egg."

"Hmm. Let's give it a shake and see if we can hear anything," suggested Uncle. "Lend a paw, there! Shaky-shake-shake!" Something inside it went click, then…

CRACK !

Suddenly it split open right down the middle and its insides flew everywhere.

It was quite a while before Fearless dared to peek out from under the bush where he and the 'kats had dived for cover. He was relieved to see that nothing was moving on the sand dune. He felt the pups pushing impatiently behind him.

"Hurry up, Uncle!" said Mimi. "I'm starving! Let's go and see if the inside of an elephant's egg is worth eating."

"We're all hungry, Mimi," snapped Uncle, "but safety first! Keep together close behind me and don't touch anything until I give the order."

The insides of the elephant-shaped shell had scattered over quite a wide area. Very cautiously, Uncle began to gather things up into a pile and inspect them. "Aha!" he announced. "Yes... I'm pretty sure all these things belong to a Blah-blah. And as you say, Skeema, this very well *could* be a mobile nursery chamber. It has spinners, after all, and all these things probably belong to a very young Blah-blah. Now, let me see if I can recognize anything."

He made a little pile.

"These," he announced importantly, "are for a youngster to chew, I think. They're not food exactly. But I've definitely seen young Blah-blahs with these in their mouths. No doubt they sharpen their teeth on them. Now, what else can I tell you about?"

"What is this?" asked Mimi. She held out a little box. Inside were a number of perfectly round smooth stones. They sparkled in the sunshine. "Look!" she gasped. "You can see right through them. Look at the lovely-colored whirly lines twisting around inside them!"

Little Dream stared at the stones. "Like eyes," he said to himself.

"I've see these hanging on the darkness in the Upworld when the suntime is gone," said Uncle. "The Blah-blahs love to watch them. They call them stars."

"They must be for the baby to watch when it hatches," said Skeema.

"Put them in the backpack," said Uncle, already turning to look at something else.

"Aha!" he exclaimed. He picked up a shiny, boxy thing. "Now this is an eye-protector, by all that crawls in damp sand! Didn't I tell you about seeing these before, in my Glory Days, when I was a young king, exploring my kingdom! Many a time the Chief of the Click-clicks bowed down in front of me. He was too nervous to look at me without protecting his

eyes—like this." Bold King
Fearless put the shiny thing in
front of his face.

"Oh, *please!*" muttered
Skeema through gritted teeth.
"He's not going to start on his
Glory Days again, is he?"

Uncle put down what he
was holding and picked up
something else. "These are interesting. I've seen
these before. I can't quite remember what they're
for. Possibly weapons of some kind." He lifted
one to his ear and shook it hard.

"Weapons? Like teeth and claws?" teased
Mimi. "Well, I must say, they look *really*
sharp... **not!**"

"Oh, well, you're probably right," said
Uncle, with a shrug. Hup! He tossed it high
into the air toward a pile of jagged rocks in a
ditch below them.

It landed. There was a mighty… **BLATT!**

…and the thing let out a hiss louder than a whole nest of cobras. It spat a long jet of evil-looking brown liquid high in the air.

Before the last of it splattered among the rocks, the little gang had scattered and lay quaking under the bush again.

"What was *that?*" gasped Skeema, his heart pounding.

"Snake-in-a-canister," said Uncle grimly. "Deadly! You give the canister a rough shake, you pull the ring on the top and the snake inside squirts a deadly poison at your enemy. I've seen the Blah-blah males practicing with these weapons sometimes at sundown."

They spread out. Cautiously, they sniffed out the other scattered contents of the shell. Nothing was moving, so they became bolder. Soon they had made another little pile.

"Hmmm! Well, now, Mimi, this (sniff-sniff) is definitely Blah-blah food," declared Uncle.

"About time!" said Mimi.

"Yum yum," said Little Dream, licking his lips.

"Can we eat now?" said Skeema. "I'm shrinking."

91

"Very well, but no fighting!" warned Uncle. "We'll share the food. Mimi, you can have this little snake with the funny nose. Little Dream can have the yellow blind-lizard. Skeema and I will share this nest of grubs."

They dug in hungrily. Mimi didn't think much of her snake. It made her mouth go all frothy.

Little Dream enjoyed his lizard, once he had bitten its head off. It was better than giant millipedes, anyway.

In spite of what Uncle had said, Skeema started a little fight to get the nest of grubs for himself. He and Uncle had a growly tug-of-war for a moment. Then the nest suddenly burst with a loud ripping sound and a shower of red, pink, blue, green, and orange grubs

flew everywhere. Uncle had to be quick to grab
some for himself. And what a disappointment!
How horribly sweet and gummy they were!
How they stuck to their back teeth!

"If this is the sort of food that Blah-blahs
eat, they can keep it! Yuck!" said Skeema,
spitting it out. The taste reminded him of some
powdery stuff he once licked off a bee's legs.
He considered stealing some of Little Dream's
lizard, but changed his mind when Little
Dream was sick on the spot.

Chapter 9

Skeema thought he had seen something jump quite a long way out of the chamber when it split open. It wasn't long before he sniffed it out. It was trying to hide under a rock, but the lime-green tail sticking out gave it away. Skeema sank his teeth into it. The creature squeaked loudly, but Skeema held on bravely and dragged it into the bright sunlight. The creature didn't move, so he got it in a death-grip and squeezed. *Squeak! Squeak!* it cried.

"That's odd," thought Skeema. "It should be dead." He nipped it all over. *Squeak! Squeak! SQUEAK!*

Uncle came over to help. "Be careful," he warned. "I have heard tales of these creatures. They live under the big water in the land of the Narrowhead meerkats. They grow into enormous monsters and their jaws go snap-snap! Have you finished him off?"

"This is amazing!" said Skeema. "He ought to be dead but he just won't give up. Watch."

He bit the creature.

It squeaked.

"I like him! He's tough! And he smells nice. I'm going to keep him as my pet," Skeema announced.

Uncle was just about to advise Skeema against this when he heard a terrified cry.

"Help!" cried Mimi. "Little Dream's climbed into the pink chamber. He says there's an enemy meerkat hiding there! I think he's having a fight!"

"It could be a Ruddertail, by all that sneaks and slides!" roared Uncle Fearless. "Take cover, you two, and don't come out of your hiding place till I give the command." He let out a blood-chilling war cry and charged toward the open shell. "Hold on, Little Dream! I'll save you!"

With one bound he leaped over the side, ready to do or die. "Have at you!" he cried, swashing away with his digging claws. And then he exclaimed, "Woa, up!" He suddenly realized that Little Dream didn't need his support. The smallest of all the Sharpeyes was locked in a life-and-death-struggle, all right.

Uncle breathed a sigh of relief. He had seen the sort of thing that Little Dream was fighting before and he wracked his brain to remember what they were called. He remembered how small Blah-blahs wandering among their pointy mounds liked to carry around little models of themselves. When they dropped them, they would pick them up, hold them tight, and call their names softly. Now, what was it they called out?

"There-there!" That was it! Little Dream had picked a fight with a There-there!

"Enemy meerkat!" panted Little Dream. "He tried to kill the Blah-blah egg." Growling fiercely, he sank his little teeth into "the enemy" again and gave him a good shake. "But he can't hurt him now!"

"Well, er, look here, good job, what-what!" said Uncle. It seemed a pity to mention that There-theres were harmless. As for the "enemy meerkat" Little Dream had fought so fiercely, it was nothing more than a reflection of himself in the There-there's dark, flat eyes. Little Dream had clearly not understood when he told him before what Blah-blah eyes looked like. Besides, Uncle remembered exactly how frightened *he* had felt when he first saw himself mirrored in the eyes of the Chief of the Click-clicks.

"Brave work, you young spitter!" said Uncle. "You've conquered your first enemy alright! You won't have any more trouble from him! Here, try his eyes on. You've earned them." He slipped them onto the proud little pup's nose and put the arms behind his ears. "Nobody will tease you about pale eye-patches now, what-what! Here, put this on too." He also slipped the strap of the eye-protector around his neck. "There! Now you look like the Chief of the Click-clicks!" he laughed.

Little Dream was amazed. "Hooray! I can see much better!" he cried and jumped up and down for joy. "I can look up at the bright sky now, look!"

Uncle interrupted. "Listen, where's this egg that you say the enemy meerkat was after?"

Little Dream pointed to something that was strapped to the other half of the chamber. It *did* seem to be some sort of egg! It was at least twice meerkat-size, in a shiny gold shell, tied with sparkling ribbon.

Uncle scratched his head. "Well, well!" he exclaimed. "So that's what Blah-blah eggs look like!"

With a *Wee-ooo-ooo-ooo!* he sounded the all-clear for Skeema and Mimi, and then quickly undressed the There-there. It looked very strange without any covering. Its body was brown and furless, and felt as hard and smooth as the walls of the pink chamber in which it traveled. It was nothing like the warm, soft, giant Blah-blah he had tamed and climbed up all that time ago. It made Uncle feel uncomfortable. He felt peculiar. There was something here he couldn't understand at all. So he solved the problem the meerkat way… by quickly burying it and forgetting about it.

He looked down at the pile of the There-there's clothes, and picked up the helmet. He tried it on. "Hmm, fits me rather well," he said to himself. "Good. I'll take these too." He put on the safari scarf and backpack and felt very handsome. "I dare say, I look pretty great!" he told himself. "Rather like a Blah-blah Chief, I imagine!"

Skeema was first to reappear, closely followed by Mimi. Little Dream was naturally very keen to show off his new eyes. He was expecting his brother and sister to be surprised, but he wasn't ready for what happened when they saw him. Their happy expressions changed to looks of alarm. They let out their wildest attack-calls. They puffed themselves out and started doing what they hoped was a fearsome war dance!

"Stand easy!" ordered Uncle, chuckling. "Relax! There's no danger! Use your noses!

It's only your little brother. Can't you smell
him?!"

Skeema and Mimi could *smell* that it was
only Little Dream, but their eyes told them
that he looked suddenly stronger, sharper,
and… well, scarier.

"What happened?" they wanted to know.

"Oh, let's just say that he was faced
with a difficult test—and he did very well,"
said Uncle. "And I for one am very proud
of him."

"Us too!" said Skeema and Mimi. They
gave him a squeeze and congratulated him.
Little Dream became shy and modestly lifted
his new eye-protector in front of his face. "No,
honestly! That was really brave, Dreamie.
Well done," they said, and meant it.

Uncle picked up the There-there's little
desert boots. "Here, these are for you,
Skeema," he said. "Wear these on your back

paws. They'll keep your claws nice and sharp and shiny, ready for action."

"Squeak!" said the lime-green Snap-snap tucked under Skeema's arm, as if he thought they looked pretty cool too.

"Mimi now, me! Me!" said Mimi.

"I have just the thing for you, my dear," said Uncle. "This piece of soft nesting material is very pretty and it will alarm your enemies. Here, wrap it around yourself."

Mimi was delighted. "Am I like a female Blah-blah?" she said to Uncle, her wide eyes shining.

"Most certainly!" said Uncle kindly. "If they have princesses among the Blah-blahs, I'm sure they look like you."

The talk of princesses made Little Dream think about their mother, Fragrant, who was taken from them before he could remember. Still, at least he and his brother and sister had Uncle Fearless to take care of them.

He put his arms around the egg. "Poor egg!" he said quietly. "What will he do without his mamma? The Vroom-vroom's gone without him!"

"Far away to the other side of the kingdom, I'm afraid," sighed Uncle.

Little Dream held his ear close to the egg. "I can hear his heart," he said.

"Let Mimi listen! Me! Me!" demanded Mimi, and pressed her ear against the shiny shell too. When they listened carefully, they could all hear the egg's heart beating. *Bic-tic-bic-tic.*

"Quick!" said Uncle. "I think we should close the chamber. We mustn't let the egg get cold." He gathered up the things that were lying about. He put all the shiny canisters into his backpack, bundled the rest of the stuff into the pink chamber next to the egg, and closed it with a snap. No sooner had he stood it up on its spinners than his ears pricked up and his eye began to dart about. He thought he heard a whispering sound from underground. Or was it the sound of loose stones tumbling down a sand dune?

"We're coming to *get* you!" came a sing-song voice; a high, pretending-to-be-a-young-meerkat voice. Then there was snickering. It sounded hollow, out of tune. It was coming from out of a bolthole that wasn't far away! "Now, what kind of far-fetched stories has that naughty old chatterbox been telling them, I wonder?" it teased.

Chapter 10

Uncle Fearless bristled and dragged the pups close to him. They could feel his growling and spit-calls vibrating through his tense body as he stood on all four paws, more like a lion than a meerkat. "I smell strangers," he whispered, and then he raised his voice into a challenge. "Show yourselves if you want a fight!"

The snickers turned to laughter. Were there three voices? "Don't worry, old timer! There's not really going to be a fight... yet!"

"Who are you? Narrowheads? What are doing so far from your own territory? Come out of your hole and face me," challenged Fearless.

"Face *us*, he means!" said Skeema, showing his teeth. "There are four fighters here!"

"Hi-yip-yip!" Mimi and Little Dream joined in. "Come on! We're not scared of you!"

Suddenly, there was a scrabbling noise and a large, gray Narrowhead male sprang up between them and the safety of the burrow entrance. At the same moment, an even larger brute leaped out from a hole hidden under a bunch of buffalo grass. There was no mistaking his misshapen silvery head or the twisted diggers on his right paw.

"Twisted Claw!" breathed Uncle.

"Hello, Fearless! So, they've left you to mind the babies and the burrow, have they? Is that all you're fit for these days—babysitting?

Dear, oh dear! Not much to brag about, is it? You used to think you were so high and mighty! Always going on about how the Blah-blahs let you climb all over them and tame them. And as for them bringing you eggs and nuts to eat! Well, we've heard a rumor that you offered *yourself* as a meal for an eagle owl! Is that right? Did you *really* stand about in the open Upworld like some sleepy little grasshopper who hasn't got a clue about keeping a proper look-out? No wonder you've only got one eye and you're a nobody! Fearless may be your name, but it's not your nature, is it? You're nothing but an old windbag!"

Twisted Claw's bodyguard threw back his ugly head and laughed like a hyena.

For a moment the strength drained out of Uncle. He glanced at the young ones and felt ashamed. What must they think of him now? The three little 'kats said nothing, but were bracing themselves for an attack. They sensed, as Uncle surely did, that the Narrowheads were softening them up.

Suddenly, Twisted Claw made a quick and secret series of whistling calls. In the flick of an eyelid, the bodyguard stopped laughing and began ducking and weaving like a snake getting ready to strike.

Faced with a half-blind old wreck of a Sharpeye and a bunch of inexperienced pups, Twisted Claw and his bodyguard would normally have walked right over them. Yet for all their outward swagger, they felt far from sure of themselves. For a start, there was something peculiar about Fearless's appearance that made them hesitate. What was that strange object on his battered head? That thick collar? The floating material around his shoulders? What was the interesting thing that he had strapped to his back like another belly?

And it wasn't only the oddness of *his* appearance that rattled them. The pups looked a bit...well, *odd* too! The female had something bright and flapping wrapped around her body. One of the young males was holding out some sort of dangerous-looking reptile in a very threatening manner. And as for the little one—what enormous scary eyes he had! Dark and square!

They only hesitated for a second, but it was enough time for Uncle to recover his wits. "Ask yourself something, Twisted Claw," he said calmly. "If I never tamed any Blah-blahs, or made them my subjects, why did they give me all this to protect my body?" He stretched out his arms to present himself in his Safari-Man outfit.

"And do you see this chamber?" He drummed it sharply with his claws. "This is a Blah-blah egg chamber. I am in charge of it."

"Yes, and we're going to take it to the Blah-blah mounds on the far side of the kingdom!" Little Dream suddenly blurted out. "We're going on an adventure. We're going to take it back to its mamma!"

Of course, Uncle wasn't expecting this. All he could do when he heard what Little Dream said was gulp and nod his head in agreement. "Er... yes. He's quite right, Twisted Claw! You're interrupting a very important... um, m-mission!" he stammered.

With that, the tables suddenly turned again. Twisted Claw puffed up his fur and became bolder. "A mission, you say? There's no need for that. Why don't we save you the trouble? Give us the chamber. We've always wanted to try taming Blah-blahs ourselves, haven't we, Patchie?"

His bodyguard nodded. "Too true!" he rumbled. "And what could be better to attract their attention than something as big and bright as this, eh?" He began to speak fast and urgently to Twisted Claw. "I reckon we should just grab it quick, Chief, because the rest of the Sharpeye mob might turn up here any minute! You flatten this crazy old windbag and leave the babies to me. They won't give us too much trouble. They're only like a bunch of little scorpions doing a crazy dance to try to scare us away, that's all."

Mimi snatched one of the shiny canisters from Uncle's backpack. "Don't you dare call me a crazy scorpion. And do not touch me, not Mimi! Not me," she shouted in a shrill voice. "I've got a deadly weapon!" She shook the canister wildly.

"So have I!!" cried Skeema, holding up his Snap-snap and squeezing it. Its piercing *SQUEAK!* shocked the Narrowheads, and they jumped back.

As it happened, there was no need for either Mimi or Skeema to test their weapons in battle. Suddenly there was a noise like the snapping of a twig and a blinding bolt of lightning shot out of Little Dream's chest!

Two more dazzling flashes quickly followed, and before the last of them faded, the terrified Narrowheads had begun to run for their lives.

"Whoops!" said Little Dream. "All I did was touch this little lump here…" There was another deadly flash that had his brother, sister, and Uncle squealing and diving for cover. "Sorry," said Little Dream, just before he fell flat on his back. "Is everybody alright?"

Chapter 11

After the group had recovered from the shock of Little Dream's daring surprise attack, they sat and talked excitedly about what had just happened.

"My goodness, Little Dream!" Uncle exclaimed with a gasp. "Whatever made you come up with that nonsense about us taking the egg chamber to the Blah-blah mounds? I nearly had a fit, what-what!"

"Sorry, Uncle," said Little Dream. "I just wanted you to be proud of me."

Uncle was touched. "I am, dear boy, I'm very proud of you. But as for traveling across the desert on our own, that's quite ridic—"

"I would like to go to Far Burrow!" interrupted Mimi. She had made up her mind. "Uncle, why *don't* we return the egg to its mother and then go and live by the Salt Pans forever and ever? I don't want to stay here with our horrid Queen Heartless."

"Me neither! I would love to see those Blah-blah mounds," agreed Skeema. "Let's all run away and go there *now!* Go on, Uncle," he pleaded. "Take us to Far Burrow. You wouldn't have to be a babysitter anymore. You could be a king again!"

"Me? A king again? You can't really suppose that…I mean to say…Come on! It's not that I've forgotten how to *be* one or anything, what-what! It's quite true that I can dish out orders and terrify the enemy as well as the next royal meerkat…"

"And you can have lots more bold adventures among the Blah-blah tribes!" squealed Little Dream. "We all can. We like adventures!"

"Well, my 'kats," laughed Uncle. "It's tempting, I must say. I'm getting ancient and rusty but you're all getting pretty bold and quick. Still, you don't know what you're asking for. You've just seen how nasty Narrowheads can be. Wait until you see the Ruddertails!"

"We're not scared of Ruddertails!" cried Skeema.

Uncle smiled and ruffled the fur on his head. "It must be true what everybody keeps saying. Just listen to us! We must all have The Madness even to *think* about making such a long journey. And there are going to be all sorts of dangers every step of the way. "

"And I don't like it here," said Mimi firmly. "I want to be in a story about how important I am."

Uncle took in a huge breath. "Right! That's settled then. We'll have no more negative nonsense! It's time to be positive. It's time to ACT! We four mad meerkats WILL travel to see the Blah-Blah mounds and we SHALL live to tell a tale or two, by all that's strong and tasty!" And to show he meant business, he lifted his tummy-pad with both paws. HUP! "And how are we going to do it?" he went on. "Altogether now!" He raised his paws above his head like a conductor.

The pups bunched together, lifted their chins high, and with one voice, they proudly spoke the words of their motto:

"Stay alert to stay alive!
And stay with the group!"

For a giggle, they pretended they were as fat as Uncle. They stuck out their tummies and lifted them up with both paws, shouting—1-2-3-HUP!

Then they got going.

Chapter 12

Fear helped the wild travelers on the first part of the journey. They ran as fast as they possibly could with a heavy egg chamber to drag along with them. Every now and then they thought they could hear scampering claws and they would turn, expecting to see the Narrowheads or perhaps some angry Sharpeyes chasing after them, but it was only the wind or the rattling of pebbles behind them. They saw neither stripe nor tail of any other meerkat.

Once they had left the dunes behind, the
ground grew hard and sloped gently down
toward The Great Plain. It was rough and
bumpy, but at least the chamber didn't keep
sinking into soft sand. In fact, now and
again, the chamber seemed to have the

power to run forward by itself like the crazy pink elephant it pretended to be.

When they reached The Great Plain, the sand grew softer again. The pups were tired and began to struggle. Uncle was very jumpy. He knew that they must push on to safer ground before they could forage for food and find somewhere to sleep for the night. There was too little cover here for his liking, and too many chances to be flattened by the blundering monsters of the Upworld—the rhinos, the herds of antelope and zebras, and the trumpeting elephants. The pups found it hard to believe that the lions, lying about in yawning, dusty-yellow heaps, were not interested in meerkat snacks. Still, nothing scared them more than snakes. The quick, black ones were the worst. And the later it got, the more every whisper of the grasses began to sound like the hiss of a lurking mamba or puff adder.

As for Uncle, the thought of attack from out of the sun made all his once-broken bones ache. He imagined that everywhere in the sky, powerful birds of prey mocked and screamed. His bent arm throbbed and there was a pain all down his side where his ribs had been shattered when he had been dropped from a great height. At least he had his helmet and his pack. They gave *some* sort of protection.

As they traveled, Uncle sang lively contact songs, expecting the young meerkats to echo the words to show that they were still there and that they were safe.

> "Look about, look about!
> (*Look about, look about)!*
> Listen out, listen out!
> (*Don't shout! Listen out!)*
> Don't know the sound?
> (*New sound! Wrong sound!)*
> Get underground!
> (*Dive underground!)*"

Uncle was right to be cautious. High in the cloudless blue, out of sight even from the keen eyes of young Skeema and Mimi, The Silent Enemy was watching.

The eagle-owl had only one thought in his revolving head: *revenge.*

The hot air lifted the eagle owl like waves holding up a swimmer in a warm sea. He kept his back to the sun and was careful not to show himself as more than a scratch in the sky. His sight was so powerful that when the meerkats were on open ground he could clearly see the sun glinting in the one busy eye that was still in Fearless's head. Each time it flashed, the eagle owl felt a twinge along his breastbone where Fearless's needle-sharp teeth had sunk in and made him scream and let go.

He knew that there is no more watchful a creature than a meerkat. But he was patient. There would be a moment when Fearless was off guard. One careless moment was all it would take, when his mind was on something else.

"Then," thought the eagle owl, "I shall drop like the darkness and dine on him! Oooo-hooo- hooo!"

When at last the worn-out travelers came to a place where devil's claw bushes, bright with yellow flowers, grew everywhere, Uncle breathed a sigh of relief. "Ground-squirrel territory!" he said. And sure enough, dozens of them popped up like little jack-in-the-boxes, flicking their charming bushy tails over their heads or swishing them out behind them. They nibbled at the yellow flowers and chattered amongst themselves.

"Can you speak their language?" Skeema asked Uncle.

"I'm afraid not," said Uncle. "But they are welcoming creatures. And we have an ancient agreement with all their tribes: we always give them shelter if they need it and they give shelter to us."

The travelers stopped and refreshed themselves, taking turns to dig for juicy roots to quench their thirst.

"Ouch!" squealed Little Dream, pricking himself on a wickedly sharp thorn for the umpteenth time. He was hungry, though, and he soon found plenty of strange-looking crawlers to fill his belly and make him forget the soreness of his nose.

And sure enough, as their shadows began to stretch, a motherly-looking ground squirrel with a broad stripe down her side led the way for them into a cool and pleasant-smelling burrow full of tumbling babies!

Chapter 13

A good sleep in the freezing darktime, snug among the soft bodies of the ground squirrel family, did the travelers good.

After a good Warm-up and a breakfast, they thanked their hosts and waved goodbye.

They struggled on, often wishing that they could leave the egg chamber behind, because it took such an effort to keep it moving. They didn't stop for rest until they came to a red ebony tree that Uncle knew well. It spread its branches widely and offered them its cool shade for rest and shelter from the sun, which was now at its hottest. Overhead, the weaver birds flitted in and out of the holes in their enormous nest, chit-chatting busily.

"Is that what the Blah-blah mounds look like?" Mimi inquired. "I can't really picture them."

"Not quite. It's hard to explain exactly how they look. But with luck, we'll see them soon enough," said Uncle. He told them a little story to try and make things clearer, but he got a bit muddled and the tale fizzled out.

Skeema felt rather sorry for him. "You know, it doesn't really matter if there's no such thing as a Blah-blah, Uncle," he said kindly. "Whatever happens, we're all together now, and that's what's important. And it's a good story, in any case!"

For once, Uncle was completely lost for words.

"I love it," murmured Little Dream sleepily.

Then the pups tumbled and fought for a short
while until they fell over, fast asleep in a heap.

When they heard the thunder of springbok
and gemsbok hooves, they twitched and
jumped up again, heads turning all around.

"They won't hurt you," murmured Uncle,
half-asleep. But his ears pricked up when he
heard the shout of jackals and the cackle of
hyenas. Suddenly, all his brave little daredevils
were burrowing under him like chicks under a
mother bird! "Far away," he said soothingly.
"Safe here."

Above them, The Silent Enemy cursed. He
had no trouble seeing the pink, lumbering
thing that the meerkats were dragging along,
but the grasses kept hiding Fearless's eye, the

one particular morsel he longed to taste more than any other. And now that the meerkats were under a tree, he could see nothing at all of the adult or the babies.

Once they had their strength back, the adventurers moved on and soon found themselves among golden grasses that whispered in the hot wind.

The spinners of the heavy chamber were useless in soft sand. The meerkats heaved, but couldn't get it to go in a straight line. It had to be pulled along a twisting path in and out among the tall tufts. For a while no one said a word, except to answer Uncle's call. No one complained about their sore paws, not even Skeema, who found that his little desert boots rubbed—but wouldn't take them off for all the ants' eggs in Africa. Little Dream did his best to keep pace with the others, though it was hard for him. Sometimes they let him ride on top of the chamber and be look-out for a while to keep his spirits up.

"You remind me of a Blah-blah female I once saw riding on a camel," said Uncle with a wink at Skeema and Mimi. "She went wibble-wobble, wibble-wobble, *squeak!*"

"Why did she go wibble-wobble squeak, Uncle?" asked Little Dream. "Was she scared?"

"Ah!" said Uncle mysteriously, putting a claw down the side of his nose to show he was telling a secret. "She didn't squeak while she was *on* the camel," said Uncle. "Only when she got off."

"But that's silly. If she wasn't wibble-wobbling any more, what did she squeak for?" Mimi wanted to know.

"I think it was because the camel spat in her eye!" said Uncle. And he laughed so much at his terrible joke that his big tummy went wibble-wobble and set the little 'kats cackling with laughter like red-billed oxpeckers.

A little fun made a tough journey seem easier. Even so, it felt like forever before Uncle said the words the pups were waiting to hear: "Not far now before we rest." He was pointing with his long, rust-tipped tail. "You see that red dune in the distance? There's a fine burrow there where we can shelter for the darktime."

But oh, what a painful "little way" that was. By the time they had dragged themselves and their heavy load to the entrance to Red Dune Burrow, they felt half-dead.

The egg chamber had to be safely buried before they could finally crawl through the main entrance and into a cool, damp, safe place. "Well done!" said Uncle, at last. "In we go then." But something made him nervous. "Wait! Stand back!" He lifted his long nose and sniffed the air.

"A cobra, by all that spits," he said softly. "Can you hear that sound like the whispering grass? He's uncoiling, what-what! That's the sound of dry scales rubbing together!"

Chapter 14

The cobra was not pleased to be disturbed.

"SSSSteer clear!" he hissed. "I'm the lord of this burrow."

"You, sir, are no such thing. You are a squatter!" shouted Uncle indignantly. "I helped to build this burrow myself long ago. Now I should like to rest and shelter here and so would these pups. Kindly slither off and find another hole."

"Mind your manners or I'll *have* you!" warned the snake. He put his head out of the burrow and looked at them with frightening eyes like small, glittering stones. His head and hood were shiny black, though when he spread out the hood to scare them, the 'kats saw that it was marked with angry red blotches. Uncle had seen cheeks swollen with poison like this before. The brute was, as Uncle's nose had told him, a zebra spitting cobra. Underground, his gray belly would be striped with glittering bands. Because he wanted to keep the burrow for himself, he was not eager to show this part of himself just yet.

"Scorpion dance," said Uncle quietly to the pups, out of the corner of his mouth. "He can't hear much but he can lip-read. Now pay attention." He turned his head slightly, without taking his good eye off the intruder in case of attack. "Stay on your toes and remember the steps. He'll be quick, so you dance quicker! Remember the snake-in-the-canister? That's how he'll go for you. He'll spit—and he can spit a long way. But if he spits, then mind your eyes! Skeema—here's the plan…"

The snake began to hiss like a burning branch in a wild fire. Though he was very deaf, he sensed that the meerkats were plotting something. His tongue flicked out, hoping to scent their fear. His jaws opened like a trap and when Skeema danced toward him, showing his teeth, he flicked his head in his direction. Skeema skipped away—and out of sight.

The cobra was well-pleased. Terror was a fine weapon. As the little female darted toward him, he pulled back again and this time sprayed twin jets of venom through his hollow fangs. The venom flew three feet, but Mimi gave a squeal and, spinning like a little furry ballerina, she pirouetted out of danger.

"Good work, Mimi! Ten out of ten for style!" cheered Uncle.

The hood was spreading again, the cheeks were swelling, and the snake was forced to slither forward. He tried to lift himself up in the confined space of the burrow and wipe the look of triumph off Uncle's face.

"Yikessssssss!" he fizzed. " What the…?"

"Has something just struck you?" inquired Uncle Fearless, innocently. He knew very well what it was that had just struck the cobra… and where. The sharp teeth of young Skeema had just locked onto his pointed backside! Uncle had sent him down and around through a side entrance to do just that.

The cobra had no room to turn back on himself, so he darted forward, his curved fangs reaching for Uncle's helmeted head. But Uncle knew the dance and stepped aside, his safari scarf swinging like a mini-matador's cape.

"Dance with *me*! With *me, again*!" cried Mimi. Furiously, the snake lunged at her. Half of him was out of the burrow now. They could see his zebra belly stripes clearly.

Meanwhile, Skeema was hanging onto his tail tightly.

"Yoo-hoo!" squeaked Little Dream. When the cobra saw a rival snake reflected in Little Dream's eye-patches, he got so angry that his jaws almost came unhinged. He leaped clear of the burrow and would have punctured the brave little pup had Uncle not taken a running jump and pushed Little Dream out of the way.

Skeema was whipped into the air by the pointed tail his teeth were locked onto. He came down on the back of the cobra's neck like a cowboy on a bucking bronco. Holding onto the hood with one paw, he gave his Snap-snap a mighty *SQUEAK!* with the other as he landed. He then pushed both sides of the hood down over the eyes of his mount, gave him one more nip on the back of the neck for luck—and then jumped sideways to the ground.

This was all too much for the intruder. With one last hiss, he gathered his coils and shot off into the falling darkness.

Chapter 15

One dry river bed usually leads to another.
For a long while there seemed no end to the
dull and dusty yellow sands before them.

But at last they came to a grayish track
that stretched out across the rolling sand hills.
They scrambled up out of the river bed and
followed this smoother way to the brow of a
hill, delighted to find that the egg chamber ran
very nicely along it on its spinners. They had
expected a long, slow haul and were surprised
to make good, quick progress.

"Not much farther now!" said Uncle cheerily. "This flat track was made by the Blah-blahs. See how wide it is, and how straight? And it has been trodden down so that they can move their Vroom-vrooms along it. Sometimes these tracks have no end, but often they lead directly to the mounds of one Blah-blah tribe or another. So stay extra sharp, what-what!" He patted Little Dream on the head. "And just keep it in mind that Vroom-vrooms can run faster than cheetahs. We must be careful. Why, I remember one time, in my Glory Days, I was wandering…"

At that moment, his words were cut off by a dreadful roar. All heads turned toward the sound and all eyes saw a cloud of dust leap just over the rise. "Take cover! Run for your lives!" yelled Uncle.

In the panic, everyone jerked the egg chamber in different directions. It tottered and crashed sideways.

"Get it over the side! Get it over the side!" yelled Uncle. "It'll be crushed!"

The pups had to overcome their instinct to dive off the road and disappear into the bush that grew thickly on either side of it. Having come this far as a team, they were all determined to be ruled by Uncle and not by blind fear.

"Hold on, Uncle! We're coming!" they cried, and gathered alongside him to put their backs into the task. But pushing an egg chamber lying on its side was much harder than pulling it upright on its spinners.

"It won't budge!" panted Skeema.

"It feels dreadfully heavy!" puffed Mimi. She dashed around to the other side and found that a long, flat stone had wedged underneath it. She got her claws under it and tried to scratch it away, but it was almost as big as she was. "There's a rock! It won't shift!"

143

she shouted. Skeema left his post and darted around to help her. Their combined efforts did the trick and they moved the stone enough for Uncle and Little Dream to feel the chamber jerk forward when they put their shoulders to it.

"It's moving! It's starting to slide!" piped up Little Dream. The roaring was getting frighteningly close, as if a herd of Kalahari lions were leaping toward them.

At last the egg chamber began to shift, inch by inch, toward the edge. Mimi and Skeema managed to grab the strap and pull with all their might while the others continued to push. Suddenly, it picked up speed and plunged to the side of the road. It reached a tipping point, wobbled—until finally it was flipped by its own weight over the edge.

Mimi and Skeema had to be quick to fling themselves out of its way into a bush, and the chamber itself crashed down and came to rest under a blue pea shrub.

Uncle had made a huge effort to save the chamber. Perhaps that was why, when it shot away from him, he fell hard onto his round belly and lay winded, unable to get up.

"Up!" said Little Dream, who had been pushing too. He tugged at Uncle's backpack. The roaring dust cloud was getting horribly close.

"No good. No puff left. Leave me. Save yourself!" panted Uncle.

Little Dream turned his head and saw his first Vroom-vroom. He just had time to consider that this was also probably the last Vroom-vroom he would ever see. It was coming at him, with its silver mouth gaping and its golden eyes lit up, as terrifying as a charging bull rhinoceros.

"Run!" ordered Uncle and closed his one eye tight. His mind was racing. *I've had my ups*

and downs, he was thinking, *but all in all it's been a good life. The pups are bright little things. They'll cope without me. And at least it'll all be over quickly...*

Still lying face down, he tried to roll himself into as small a ball as possible and put his paws over his ears.

All of a sudden, he felt teeth tugging at the
fur on the back of his neck and found himself
being dragged, not toward the edge of the
track, but toward the middle.

It flashed through his mind that he had been grabbed by a jackal or a bat-eared fox and he struggled, weak as he was, to shake himself free. Then he was astonished to hear a voice he knew very well (though it came through teeth firmly clamped together) calling, "I've got you, Uncle!"

Fearless opened his eye and turned his head just enough to be able to see that it was Little Dream who had hold of him!

"Stop, Dreamie! Let go of me!" he panted. The little meerkat seemed to have found enormous strength. "Wrong way!" he tried to tell him. "Save yourself!"

His voice was lost in the thunder of the engine sound.

Then the Vroom-vroom ran over them both.

Chapter 16

Mimi and Skeema were too stunned to move. They lay under a bush, sobbing in each other's arms, long after the thunder of the Vroom-vroom had become an angry hum and faded into the distance.

"My Uncle! My Dreamie!" wailed Mimi. "What am I going to do without them?"

"What about me?" sniffed her brother. "They were mine, too, you know!"

"Go up and see what's happened to them. I can't bear to look," said Mimi. A horrible picture of a dead porcupine she had seen further down the track flashed into her mind. It had been squashed flat to twice its normal size.

"Me? What makes you think that I want to see them... like that!" snapped Skeema. He grabbed her paw. "Come on. We've got to make sure, but let's go and look together."

The thorns of the thick bushes into which they'd thrown themselves were devilishly sharp. They had to be careful to pick their way out and into the open. They were both expecting to have to face the worst sight they could ever imagine. So it wasn't surprising that for the moment, Skeema forgot part of the Sharpeye motto: *Stay alert to stay alive.* That was the last thing on his mind as he scrambled up to the top branch of a tree and forced himself to peep down at the road.

At once, relief flooded through him, sweeter than scorpion-juice. He saw by some miracle— large as life and completely unhurt—dear old Uncle Fearless sitting up in the road while Little Dream fanned him with his helmet!

As it happened, it was almost the last thing he saw. From the cloudless sky above them, a wicked shadow was swooping with no sound, no warning. It dropped more swiftly than

the cold darktime that blots out the sun.

It was The Silent Enemy.

Luckily, Mimi had her wits about her. One danger can hide another and her keen eyes had spotted one. She let out an ear-splitting alarm call and knocked Skeema off his lookout post. They tumbled headlong through thick, spiky branches to the ground.

They both screamed with terror and braced themselves. At any second, each expected to be snatched from under the bush and hoisted into the air by a wicked bunch of dagger-sharp talons.

Out on the open road there were other yells and shrieks. These were followed by the eagle owl's hoot of triumph. A terrible silence followed. Then came Little Dream's defiant, "Take that, you big bully!" The eagle owl made one more dreadful, gargling sound and suddenly, Mimi and Skeema could see him through the tangle of leaves and branches above them! They watched the great bird struggling to take off with a wild flapping of wings that shook feathers off of him like rain.

He seemed to be choking and spinning clumsily around. They could see his yellow eyes were wide with terror as he battled to lift himself into the air.

"Oh no!" thought Skeema, and tried to cover his sister's eyes with his paw. "He's got somebody in his claws!"

For a few more seconds, the wicked bird zigzagged and staggered just above the ground until, with a great effort, it heaved itself into the sky and was gone.

Skeema and Mimi hugged one another and trembled, not knowing what to do.

"Wheeee!" came a loud voice from above. Almost immediately, there was a crash as something dived into the bush they were hiding under.

"Is it the eagle owl? Has he come back for us now?" shrieked Mimi.

Another crash, louder than the first, followed by a shout. "Missed us, what-what!"

Branches were bent and snapped, leaves were smacked, and twigs cracked—but not by The Silent Enemy.

"By all that roars and hoots, those were two close calls!" yelled Uncle, brushing sand out of his fur and straightening his collar, safari scarf, and helmet. "I was certain I was no better than roadkill when the Vroom-vroom came charging at us," he panted, "but Little Dream here had different ideas, what-what!"

"I could see the spinners on the Vroom-vroom," gasped Little Dream. "They were fixed on each side, throwing up dust and stones. Still, I could see a gap between them and I *just* managed to drag Uncle into it. The Vroom-vroom ran right over the top of us but the spinners missed us completely! But, oh gosh! Then we saw The Silent Enemy."

"Oh, and he thought he'd got me for sure this time—the coward! The sneak! The snake-in-the sky!"

"We saw him grab you, Uncle," said Mimi. "We thought we'd never see you again!"

"Well, unluckily for him, all he got was my backpack!" said Uncle with a laugh. "Ha-ha! That'll be a tasty treat for him, don't you think?"

"Thank goodness you're both *alive*!" gasped Skeema, giving his dear old Uncle a hug and a warm, wet scent-mark on both cheeks. "We thought you were both..." He managed to grab his little brother and give him bit of a hug, too. *A cheek-mark would be a bit much*, he thought, but he gave him a good squeeze and a warm, brotherly pat on the back.

"Well, here we are, nearly dead, but not quite," said Uncle, who was starting to feel better already. "And all thanks to Little Dream."

"But it was you who taught me to keep a sharp look-out!" Little Dream piped up.

"Yes, well, that's kind of you to say so. But you kept your head! There's the thing. And you saved us both, by all that's sharp and lively!"

"What did he do, exactly?" asked Mimi.

"Well, there we were," said Uncle in his story-telling voice. "Me and this courageous little squirmer, both flat out in the road, me on my tummy and Dreamie on his back. I couldn't see a blessed thing. The dust from the Vroom-vroom was terrible! So there I was, blinded and thrashing about like a helpless 'kat. Not a chance of spotting The Silent Enemy, of course. So he obviously thought— *Good show! Meerkat on the menu. Dive, dive, dive!"*

"But Dreamie saw him!" Skeema could picture it now.

"Thanks to my Blah-blah eyes," said Little Dream, modestly. "They let me look right into the sun if I want to!"

"He spotted the enemy alright! And quick as a cricket, he got his paw in my backpack. He felt around for the little box—and before you knew it, he'd grabbed one of the shiny round stars belonging to the baby Blah-blah."

"Ah! Did you hurl it at him? Did you clonk him on his horrid beaky head with it?" asked Mimi, thinking that's just what she would have liked to do. "Craftier than that!" cried Uncle. "He held it in the flat of his paw and made it flash in the sunlight. That idiotic bird couldn't believe his luck! He thought *at last* he had the chance to grab the good eye I got away with last time he attacked me! But Little Dream had laid the perfect trap for him and he fell for it! You could say…" said Uncle, wiping tears of mirth from his eye as he laughed at his own joke, "…you could say he *swallowed the thing whole*, what-what! Ha-ha! Hee-hee! And let's hope he jolly well chokes on it!"

"Little Dream!" cried Mimi. "What a big, brave meerkat you are!" She grabbed him and danced him off his paws.

"Brilliant!" cried Skeema. "And I thought I was the cunning one in our family!"

"Brilliant is the word!" chuckled Uncle. "So that blasted bird won't be bothering us again

158

anytime soon." He shivered with relief. "Gosh, what a scare!" He gave himself a good shake to clear his mind.

"Plenty of scares! That's what we all need!" said Mimi, joining in, shaking herself until her fur stood out like a mad little duster.

"Hear! Hear!" said Skeema with a giggle, before joining in like a wet puppy and shaking himself all over, too.

That night, having found a burrow to sleep in, Uncle insisted on a group grooming session before bedtime to get rid of the ticks they'd picked up on the journey.

After that, feeling very proud of everyone, Uncle kept watch under the stars for a time, while the youngsters slept safely below.

Chapter 17

The hills that had been in the misty distance
for much of the journey were solid and up-
close by next suntime. After the scare with the
Vroom-vroom they decided not to risk keeping
to the road. That meant a lot of hard work
to keep the egg chamber rumbling forward.
The grasses grew greener and more lush and
the scrub was thicker now. Still, excited about
getting close to their goal, the little mob
pushed on in good spirits.

They hadn't gone far when Mimi pointed out
something hanging from the highest branch of

a tall tree. "Look! It's your backpack, Uncle!" she cried. "Let me get it down for you!"

Mimi darted up the tree, agile as a monkey. "It *is* your backpack, Uncle!" she called down. "The Silent Enemy must have been disappointed that he wasn't clutching *you* in his claws! Wow—what a view from here!" She gasped. "I can see right across the valley to where it gets all gray and as flat as flat again!"

"The Salt Pans," chuckled Uncle. "I thought as much!"

"And look! There!" came Mimi's call again. She pointed and her tail-flag started waving as if it had The Madness in it. "I can see something interesting. Some sort of pointy termite mounds, I think!"

The others left the egg chamber where it was and scrambled up to her swaying perch to join her. "You're right!" said Uncle. "Those

161

mounds are *very* interesting. But you won't find many termites in them!"

Suddenly he was clutching at all the little meerkats and pulling them to him. His chin wobbled. It took him a little moment to be able to speak, and then he said quietly, "I know you must think I'm a bit of an old phony. And I have to admit that I can lay it on a bit thick about my Glory Days. I wouldn't blame you at all if you had made up your minds that everything I said about the Blah-blahs was just stories. But listen. You're now looking at something you'll be able to tell your own pups about one day. Right now, we are looking at some real, live, actual... Blah-blahs!"

The 'kats were struck dumb with wonder. They watched in astonishment as groups of charming giant creatures ventured out and moved on their hind legs among their strange,

flapping, dwelling places. They could see
they were gigantic, even from a distance, and
naked-looking, not having any fur, but for
all their strangeness, they behaved just like
meerkats in lots of ways! They dashed about
together in family groups, slipping in and out
of their pointy mounds. Then suddenly, they
were chattering and jumping up and down in
an excited mob, pointing and calling *Oolook-
look!* at something in the sky.

"Aren't they *funny*! Aren't they *cute*!!" cried
Little Dream.

"They must have spotted those pink ibises
and woolly-necked storks flying by!" laughed
Skeema. "Oh! Silly things! They must think
they're dangerous! They've put up those flappy

warnings to scare them off. And look at the way they hide their eyes behind their little shiny boxes!"

"So *sweet* with their big monkey faces!" cooed Mimi. "How I'd love to hug one and stand on its head! Are they from the Oolook tribe, Uncle?" asked Mimi.

"I can't tell you until we get closer," said Uncle with a shrug. "I'm afraid they all look the same to me from here." Then he pointed a little to the left at a lovely sandy spot deep in the valley, not far from a group of the tallest, greenest trees they had ever seen. Their sheltering branches spread like umbrellas and made shadows as cool and inviting as underground chambers.

"That is Shepherd Tree Clump," said Uncle, with a lump in his throat. "And under that beautiful white sand—do you see? That's Far Burrow. That's where we're heading. That's our new home."

They stood for a moment, eyes glistening, swaying in the branches, without a care in the Upworld.

Then Skeema stiffened. He'd seen something. "Oh, no! We're not the only ones heading for Far Burrow by the look of it!" he said in dismay.

He pointed out something moving stealthily down through the grass tufts on the orange dunes on the other side of the valley.

"Oh no! By all that's impudent!" exclaimed Uncle. "It can't be…! Not this side of the Salt Pans, surely!"

Chapter 18

"My eye's not good enough to be sure at this distance, darn it! And those creatures are well beyond scenting range," growled Uncle. "Mimi. How about you, my dear? Can you make out their markings? I hope to goodness I'm mistaken and they're no more our enemies than ground squirrels."

"It's not easy to tell exactly what they are from here," said Mimi. "They keep low and then dash from tuft to tuft."

"Cunning," murmured Uncle. "Lined or striped?"

"I can see one," exclaimed Skeema. "There he goes… and he's striped!"

"I've got him," said Mimi. "Look how orange they are. Aha! I get it! That's how they can stay hidden against the dunes."

"Check the tails," urged Uncle.

"There's nothing bushy about them," said Mimi. "They're skinny and upright, most of them, very long and with dark red at the tip, not black like ours."

"Then it's as I feared. Those are Ruddertails!"

"Look! There are three more over there, by that bush," said Little Dreamer making the branch quiver as he pointed.

"I'll bet they're heading for The Grove," muttered Uncle. He was thinking of the thick hedge of plants where herds of antelope came to feed in the dry season. Now they were covered in pink and white flowers.

"The Ruddertails think they can keep out of sight there and then move together among the shepherd trees," he told the others. "That way they'll be close enough to the burrow to see whether it's already occupied. I expect they'll lie low in the boltholes in the darktime and then prepare a surprise attack just after Warm-up. They'll note how many of the rightful owners come out to forage. Then once they're confident that they have the greater number—Vrrrrr!—they'll pounce!"

"An ambush, eh? So what's your plan, Uncle?" asked Skeema.

"Well, in my day the usual tactic was to bring up the whole tribe to dance in front of the burrow—show the enemy our teeth and claws, what-what! But…"

"But what, Uncle?" asked Mimi. She liked the idea of a face-to-face scrap.

"The trouble is, we won't have a lot of teeth and claws to show them. There could easily be ten times more of them," said Uncle with a sigh. "We wouldn't stand a worm's chance!"

Skeema turned to look at his brother and saw himself reflected in his shiny new eyes. He liked what he saw and puffed out his fur. "I've got an idea," he said. "If the Ruddertails are planning to give us a little surprise, then maybe we should…"

Little Dream finished his sentence for him: "…give them an even bigger surprise!" he cried.

Chapter 19

The plan the group came up with meant that they had to move quickly. Before anything useful could be done to defend it, they must quickly claim the burrow and scent-mark the territory around it before the enemy arrived.

Dragging the egg chamber through the thick scrub was painful. There were roots and scratchy branches everywhere. Panting like wild dogs, the adventurers arrived at last at the lip of the steep valley and looked down toward the leafy greenness below.

They could clearly see the low, sandy mounds that marked the entrances and escape tunnels. The problem now was that there was no cover. Hardly anything grew on the dry, stony slope that led down to Far Burrow and its splendid foraging grounds.

"Even a mole-snake would be able to spot us if we started pulling a pink baby elephant down there!" groaned Skeema. "We wouldn't have a hope of surprising the enemy."

"You're right. We'll have to bury the egg chamber here and collect it after the battle," said Uncle. They opened it to check that the egg was safe. Mimi pressed her ear against it, making its shiny covering rustle. "I can still hear its heart beating," she said. "But it's very faint." *Bic-tic-bic-tic!* it went. She gave it a squeeze to warm it a bit.

The egg made a whirring sound and suddenly cried out in a strange sing-song voice:

"Happy birthday to you
Happy birthday to you!
Happy birthday, dear Charlie,
Happy birthday to you!"

Mimi was so shocked, she fell flat on her back. The others dived for cover. When the egg made no sign of speaking again, they crept back.

"What do you think, Uncle?" asked Little Dream.

"I think it must be about to hatch into a Blah-blah," said Uncle. "How strange! I had no idea that they could talk while they're still in their shells! But we haven't time to wait. We have a battle to fight and we must get into position, what- what! We'll just have to cover the egg to keep it warm and come back for it as soon as we can."

Quickly, he checked the weapons in his backpack. "Mimi, you'll take these snake-in-the-boxes. Skeema, see what you can do with these." He rattled the star-stones in their little box. Then he noticed something lying in the open egg chamber. "I'll take this black stick

cLIcK!

and sharpen my teeth on it," he said, and put it into his mouth while he and the others snapped the egg chamber shut and covered it in leaves and branches.

"Nga-nga," said Uncle, meaning to say, "*Well done*," but forgetting he had his mouth full. Suddenly, a blinding light shot out from the end of the stick. The pups squealed and covered their eyes. Uncle nibbled again. The light went out. Nibble—on. Nibble—off.

"Marvelous!" he said. "A sun-stick—that's dazzling! This will give those Ruddertails something to think about!" He slipped it into his backpack and looked at the little meerkats, who were determined, but understandably nervous. "What we are about to face may easily be the greatest challenge of our lives. So listen while I go over the battle plan."

Chapter 20

As expected, the full company of the Ruddertails arrived soon after the sun lit up Shepherd
Tree Clump. They were led by King Leaper.
He was, as Uncle had warned, even bigger
and more cruel-looking than Twisted Claw. A
vivid stripe seemed to split his domed skull in
two and his jaw opened and closed ceaselessly,
displaying long, deadly fangs. His eye-patches
ran into deep, black, narrow caves from his
twitching nostril to his tattered ears. His
movements were always quick and threatening
and his deep, staring eyes challenged everything

in their view. Leaper moved among his restless troops as they presented themselves straight after Warm-up under the spreading branches of their gathering place. Briskly, he scent-marked all his followers, never pausing until all thirty-seven of them carried his powerful stink. To judge by the grunt of pride that each Ruddertail gave as they were squirted, he might as well have been dressing them in bite-proof armor.

"Ruddertails! Show your rudders!" cried Leaper, and at once a forest of red-tipped tails rose like bloody spears. They bustled about like a moving stockade, screaming and dancing. Then they rushed forward until they were not much more than a leopard's leap from the main entrance to Far Burrow.

What stopped them was a small, feeble-looking little female. She stepped out from the shadowy mouth of the burrow and boldly blocked the entrance with her skinny body. The Ruddertail army hooted with laughter and screamed insults. They waved their tails, made little pretend charges, and hopped up and down menacingly. They were a bit worried by the colored material she had wrapped around her— but there were so many of them, they felt sure they could soon shoo her away like a spider.

To their surprise, the strange little thing took no notice at all. Instead, she stood alone in the bright sun, calmly lifted her tummy— HUP!—and warmed herself. The noise and the war dancing grew louder and wilder. She simply smiled and waved at them as if they were friends and then began to hop and skip about. She dug a little play-mound (which she jumped on and off) then she did a roly-poly and sang quietly to herself.

The Ruddertails grew frantic and stampeded about. But since the little meerkat did not seem

177

the least bothered, they gradually ran out of puff. Finally they slowed down to a gentle jog. "Hold your positions, Ruddertails!" came the commanding voice of King Leaper. "Save your energy! Can't you see that this little meerkat is too crazy or stupid to be frightened? Leave her be and stand by until we see exactly what kind of army the enemy can bring out to challenge us! Wait for my signal to charge."

Mimi was pleased with the way things had gone so far. Next, she took off her dress and tied it to a stick. As the breeze picked up, it began to flicker and crack in the breeze like the flags that the Blah-blahs flew over their pointy mounds. As soon as Mimi planted the stick in the sand, it came to life once more. It shimmered a brightly-colored warning. "Do not touch me!" it seemed to say. "I am an unknown enemy. Bite me and my poison will make you scream."

"Oo-er! W-w-what's she doing?" a nervous young Ruddertail asked his neighbor.

"I dunno!" came the anxious reply. "But I don't like the way that flat creature looks at you! And listen to him snapping. That's dangerous, that is!"

Mimi then dug just below the mound she had made and uncovered two canisters...

"Now what?" came the worried voice.

"What are those two shiny things she's dug up?"

Mimi batted them about and rolled them gingerly. Then, she grabbed one between her teeth and shook it wildly. She dropped it, backed away, crept up to it, put her ear against it, and let out a piercing scream, "Spit, cobra, spit!"

It was a dreadful noise and the Ruddertails all shuffled back a little when they heard it. They turned to their king, not knowing what

to do next. Then they saw Mimi hook a claw
under the ring at one end of the canister. It
gave a frightful *HISSSSS!* and shot
brown venom toward them. As one body,
the attackers shrank back with howls of fear.
It took all Leaper's courage to stay where
he was. He knew that if he turned tail now,
with the whole tribe expecting him to set an
example, his days as king would soon be over.

"We must push forward!" he cried. "She may strike some of us with her poison, but the rest of us will win! We need to get into the burrow quickly and chase out any Sharpeyes who are sheltering underground."

"Come on, then!" shouted one of his braver followers. "Forward, the Ruddertails!"

But before a charge could begin, another young Sharpeye warrior (Skeema—who else?) rushed out of the burrow, with a growl that was more like a leopard cub's than a meerkat's. Was he about to do battle with the Ruddertails? No! He was preparing for a fight with something deadly-looking! A nasty, lime-green Snap-snap, it was. It went for his front leg! What a struggle! Suddenly, the young meerkat flipped the Snap-snap high in the air and sank his teeth into its neck as it came down. It let out an ear-splitting *SQUEAK!*

"He's killed it!" cried one of the Ruddertails. He was so impressed, he blurted out, "Well played, son!" and got promptly nipped by his fellow soldiers.

The young Sharpeye sniffed the Snap-snap and lifted it up in his paws to mark his victory. Then—horror of horrors—the Snap-snap suddenly came to life again! It wriggled, it jumped high in the air! As it came down, the youngster tried to catch it, but it opened its terrible jaws and clamped them around his throat! The Ruddertails were shocked into silence as they watched the young Sharpeye fighting to save himself again. They half-hoped he would hold on—but suddenly his legs gave way. He slipped. Slowly the Snap-snap tightened his jaws. Bit by bit, he squeezed the breath out of the brave young struggler until he flopped lifeless onto the sand. He gave a final twitch and lay still. The Snap-snap's victory squeak was enough to make the blood run cold. But there was something really wicked about the way it suddenly flew up into the air, did a somersault, and dived straight back down the entrance to the burrow.

"Bull's-eye!" muttered Skeema to himself, pleased with his rather lucky throw. Then, it was time for a bit more acting. "ARRGHHH!" he gurgled, very theatrically. "My paws!" he yelled, howling with pain. He went wild. He jittered and squirmed all over the sand. Then he sat up—and pulled off his desert boots!

There was shock among the Ruddertail ranks. "He's pulled his back feet off!" someone yelled. "I don't believe it! He's pulled 'em right off! And now look! He's chucking them up in the air!"

Not content with tearing off his own feet, he put his front paws up to his eyes—and pulled them out! He actually pulled out his shiny

round eyes and flung *them* into the air. The
sun caught them and made them sparkle for a
second before they plopped into the sand with
two sickening thuds.

"Errr!" chorused the Ruddertail army.
"Disgusting!"

They watched open-mouthed as the poor
fellow wriggled to the entrance hole and slid
himself down it. There followed another awful
scream.

"That Snap-snap must have finished him
off!" gasped an old-timer. "That poor little
guy killed it, but then it came back to life!
Then it poisoned him and sent him raving
mad! And now it's finished him off!"

"I'm *definitely* not going down that burrow!
Not with a spitting cobra *and* a Snap-snap
down there!" replied his neighbor.

The king sensed the rising panic amongst
his soldiers. "Keep your nerve, everyone!" he

called. "Stand by to rush the burrow. We don't know for sure how many of them there are, but there can't be many. On the count of three, we'll charge together. Are you all set? One… two…"

At the count of two, a *very* small meerkat with square, shiny black eyes came charging out of the entrance to the burrow and ran straight at them. At first, he seemed to be all on his own. Instead of the normal war cry, he shouted, "Wheeee!," as if he were having the time of his life.

"Tear him to pieces!" commanded Leaper. The Ruddertails flew toward him as one, teeth and claws at the ready. But the fact was, as they closed on Little Dream and looked into his eyes, he suddenly turned into a whole army with a forest of tails waving. Dozens of meerkats had suddenly appeared out of thin air, dancing and threatening!

The front rank of the Ruddertails staggered to a ragged halt, turned, and ran into the ones behind. "What's the matter with you all? CHARGE!" screamed King Leaper.

That was the signal for yet more Sharpeye fighters to pop up from escape holes all around the burrow, dancing and yelling for all they were worth. Amazingly, the crazy little female was there again, another snake-weapon in her paw. The young male who had pulled out his eyes and torn off his feet had come back to life too! He was running along clutching the poisonous Snap-snap.

"Don't hang back, you fools!" screamed the King of the Ruddertails. "There are far more of us than them. CHARGE!"

The Ruddertail army was well-drilled and used to obeying orders. The warriors were nervous and upset, but still they gathered

themselves into their fighting formation and prepared to rush the enemy. But once again, a wicked, hissing snake sprang from the tube the little female was holding and spat great gobs of sticky brown poison high into the air. At the same time, a bolt of lightning flashed from the chest of the littlest meerkat. How the Ruddertails howled and panicked! And when they uncovered their faces and looked up, they saw a sight not one of them would forget.

Chapter 21

A beast was charging down the side of the valley, trumpeting and raising a cloud of dust.

"An elephant!" someone yelled. "A pink elephant on the charge!"

"Look out!"

"Retreat! Head for the dunes! Take cover! Run for your lives!"

Uncle Fearless could only cling onto the galloping egg chamber. He was going in the right direction and he was doing a good job making trumpeting noises, but had no control over his mount. To tell the truth, it wasn't part of the plan for it to gather *quite* so much speed. By the time it hit the mound in front of the back entrance to Far Burrow, it was racing like a cheetah.

The egg chamber roared up the steep slope and took off. There was a moment's hush as it hung in the air...then slammed into the middle ground between the two armies—and burst open.

The egg that Uncle and the pups had wanted so much to return to its mamma was jerked free of its straps and rolled among the enemy warriors. Several of the Ruddertails were bowled over by it, like furry bowling pins. As the egg bounced along, the golden covering and the ribbon around it were ripped away.

Suddenly a monstrous creature was hatched! As it broke from its golden, shiny shell, it was already flapping and calling a wild *Ooo-hoo-hoooo!*

It was an eagle owl!

Not one Ruddertail stayed around to see
what happened next, but the young 'kats saw
it. Caked in dust and bruised all over, Uncle
staggered to his feet. Blink as he might, he
couldn't clear the muck from his one good eye.
Dimly, he saw the moving wings of… The
Silent Enemy. He heard repeated the chilling
HOO-HOOO of his attack-call. Until now,

this sound had always made Fearless tremble and turned his insides to jelly. Yet now he felt nothing but rage.

"So, you have come back for the pups!" he cried. "You think you can take them when their minds are busy with thoughts of the Ruddertails! But you'll have to get past me first, what-what!"

Furiously he leapt at his arch-enemy, exclaiming, "Do your worst with your nasty beak and talons! This time, we fight to the death!" And with that, he grabbed the eagle owl and shook the daylights out of him! Feathers and fluff and stuffing flew, but Fearless the Bold battled on, ripping and twisting.

"*We love you, Charlie!*" sang the eagle owl in two voices that sounded like Blah-blah calls.

"Aha! Not so silent now, are you?" yelled Uncle.

"Happy birthday to our best little boy," said the voices of the eagle owl. "We hope you have a wonderful holiday and see lots of meerkats!"

Uncle wasn't put off by this frightening, meaningless babble. He never gave up the struggle until he had the hard, dark heart of his arch-enemy in his jaws.

HOO
HOO!

Even then, it seemed determined to have a last word:

"Happy birthday to you,"

sang the heart.

"Happy birthday to you
Happy birthday, dear Charlie
Happy b–"

One final crunch from Uncle's fiercely gritted teeth—and it was silenced forever.

Chapter 22

None of the fighters caught up in the battle noticed, but a party of Blah-blahs had been filming the whole thing. Apart from the cameraman and the soundman, there was a TV presenter, his wife, and their little boy.

As the last of the screaming Ruddertails galloped back beyond the Salt Pans, never to return, the watchers stepped out of their hiding place and looked with amazement at the wreckage on the battlefield.

"I say!" gasped the woman. "You said we might see a bit of action, but—my goodness!—

that was extraordinary!" She turned to the little boy. "Wasn't it, Charlie, dear? Aren't you glad we came to see Daddy at work? And on your birthday, too!"

The little boy at her side put his thumb in his mouth and nodded. She picked him up and hugged him.

"Did you get all that, guys?" the presenter asked the film crew. "I hope so, because that was the most amazing behavior we've seen so far!"

"Don't worry, it's all on film," said the cameraman, whose name was Nick. "How was the sound, Jack?"

"It was all too far away to hear much," said the soundman. "But I'll play some of it back." He flipped a switch and it was just possible to hear a tinny voice singing *Happy birthday to you...*

"How very strange!" said the woman in a shocked whisper. "Feedback, I suppose..."

Her husband wasn't paying attention though. He had stooped and picked something up. "Do you know, sweetheart," he said, "some of these things scattered around look just like Charlie's! This flashlight, for example." He explored a little further and picked up something else. "And look here! Here's a glass marble. Charlie had a little collection in a matchbox, remember? And here's a picture book and an opened packet of jelly beans! Well I never! This is exactly like the stuff we packed in Charlie's suitcase."

"Yes, but darling, the suitcase fell off the roof of the Jeep somewhere *miles* from here. You remember? When we got caught in that sandstorm on our way back to camp and got completely lost?"

"Daddy! Look over here!" wailed Charlie, pointing down the other side of the sand dune he was standing on top of. "Somebody broke my elephant case!" And he burst into tears.

"Oh, don't cry on your birthday, Charlie! We'll get you another suitcase to keep your things in," soothed his mother.

The presenter was bending over something else he had discovered. "Well, now this is just *incredible*! Look what I've just found. It's the remains of the SPEKE-TO-ME eagle owl toy we bought Charlie as a birthday present! It's been ripped to shreds. What a pity! After all the trouble we took to record a heartbeat and a birthday message! Here's the speaker, look—and the batteries. I'm afraid one of the meerkats must have thought it was the real thing and attacked it!"

"That's not surprising when you remember that the eagle owl is one of the meerkat's most successful predators," his wife reminded him.

"What *is* surprising is that all Charlie's belongings have turned up here!"

Charlie looked blankly at the mess and his sobs turned to a sniffle. Something had caught his attention. Flying from a stick planted on a little heap of sand was the ragged piece of soft, colored cloth. Once it had been Mimi's dress and now it was a battle flag.

Charlie's round, angry face lit up at last. His mouth stretched into a proper birthday smile. "MY NOO-NOO!" he beamed, and snatched it into his arms.

He scrunched his long-lost blanket softly against his cheek, sat down, and closed his eyes. Bliss!

His mommy and daddy came and sat down beside him. They looked at each other and smiled. "I think that's probably the best birthday present you've ever had, isn't it, Charlie?" the woman said. Their little boy nodded, his eyes still tight shut with happiness.

Meanwhile, his dad had noticed that one of the meerkats was stretched out on the battlefield. It lay quite still. "What a shame!" he said to himself. "I hope he's not too badly hurt." Quietly, he made his way toward it.

When the man was just a step away, Uncle Fearless began to stir. His whiskers twitched, he blinked, and he rolled onto his side.

"Hush!" whispered the presenter, placing his finger to his lips to warn the others. "This poor old meerkat must have been knocked cold. I think he's just beginning to come around." He lifted his camera to his eye and looked through the viewfinder at the dazed creature. "I'd like to get some close-ups. Don't make any sudden moves now or you'll frighten him."

Charlie stayed where he was and his mother knelt down in the sand beside him.

"Well, I'm blessed!" exclaimed the presenter softly. "This is quite astonishing! All this time I thought we'd lost the dear old boy—and here he is!" He signaled to his wife to bring the boy over to look. "This is His Majesty!" he whispered. He was obviously very moved. "The star of *Meerkats on the Move*! He's definitely the dominant male we spent such a long time filming for our last series. He's still wearing the radio collar I put on him, can you see?"

Tenderly he slid his hand under the cheek of the dazed little creature. What he saw clearly upset him. "Oh dear, the poor old fellow's face has been horribly injured, look. Can you see? He's lost one of his eyes. It looks like an old injury. He really has been through the war, poor fellow. I do hope he's not going to slip away just when we've found him again."

"Are you sure that's His Majesty?" whispered his wife.

"I'm certain. I recognize him from the pattern of patches on his back. Come over here, Nick. Bring the camera, nice and steady. Jack, bring the microphone closer." Gently he stroked Fearless's cheek with his finger. Come on, old soldier. See if you can get up on your feet. It's me. Don't you remember me?" He made a click-click sound with his tongue. That did it! The meerkat twitched. All his senses jerked into action. He whipped his head around and opened his good eye.

"Blah-blahs!" said Fearless to himself. He saw how they bowed down to him and hid their faces behind their eye-protecting boxes. "And I'd know that call anywhere!" He gazed up at the presenter. "Well, well! If it isn't my old friend and helper, the Chief of the Click-clicks!"

"Thank goodness!" exclaimed the presenter, as softly as he could when he was so excited. "He's coming around and I think he knows me! He doesn't seem at all afraid."

Uncle pulled himself to his full height and gave himself a shake. He turned and caught the scent of the pups in their hiding places and called for them to follow. Boldly and steadily, Uncle began to climb the leg of the presenter. The eyes of the wife and the child grew wide with wonder. They both stood up to watch.

"*Di-deet!*" called Uncle, and Skeema and Mimi threw caution to the wind and came dashing along to do as he instructed. While Uncle clambered right up on top of the Blah-blah's head, the pups chose a slightly lower perch on his shoulders.

"It's all true!" said Mimi, excitedly. "You really can get the Blah-blahs to obey you!"

"I always knew it was true about your Glory Days," said Skeema. "Anyone can see you're a real king and not just a pretend, secret one. And isn't it a wonderful view from up here, Dreamie?" He looked down for his brother but for a moment he couldn't see him.

Suddenly there was a cry of delight from the little boy. "Mommy! Mommy! Look what the littlest meerkat's doing! He's climbing up onto my head!" Charlie wasn't at all afraid. "Hello, little meerkat!" he whispered, and reached up to give his tummy a tickle.

His mother's face lit up with a broad smile and all the meerkats had to hold tight as their human look-out posts shook with laughter.

"I love Far Burrow," cried Little Dream with a delighted laugh, as everyone curled up together in a freshly dug chamber, safe and cool in the darktime. "Is it ours now?"

"Well we won it, didn't we?" chuckled Uncle. "By hook *and* by crook, what-what!"

"And you can be King of the Sharpeyes again as well as King of the Blah-blahs!" said Skeema.

"Um, yes—well—look here!" said Uncle. "I for one should be delighted to start again, with my own little tribe. In which case, I really think we need to give ourselves a new name. Has anyone got any suggestions?"

Little Dream did have a suggestion, and a very good one.

And as the shepherd trees began to throw cool shadows across the entrance to their beautiful new burrow, a delighted little crowd of Click-clicks was huddled happily together around a computer. They were enjoying the first screening of a scene that would soon be shown all around the world. In it, a famous presenter was telling the viewers, with pride and delight, that his wife and little boy were privileged to be the very first look-out posts of a brand-new meerkat clan.

"This delightful, brave old creature," he whispered, "is a very long way from his old home. He has clearly suffered a dreadful injury, and may well have lost his place as leader of the Sharpeyes. But I'm happy to report that he's alive and well. And it looks very much as if he intends to start, here on the edge of the Salt Pans, a new life, with a brand new tribe…"

And of course he was right.

And for their fans all over the globe, here is the latest family picture of…

The Really Mad Mob.